EGYPTIAN CHRONICLES

THE DEATH STALKER

Hopi and Isis can remember the terrible accident on the River Nile, when they lost their parents to crocodiles. Hopi still bears crocodile teethmarks on his leg. But five years have passed, and they've been lucky: eleven-year-old Isis is a beautiful dancer, and she's been spotted by a dance and music troupe in the town of Waset. Now they live with the troupe, and Isis performs regularly. Meanwhile, thirteen-year-old Hopi, marked by the gods, pursues his strange connection with dangerous creatures . . .

Join them in the world of ancient Egypt as they uncover the dark deeds happening around them. If there's anything you don't understand, you may find an explanation at the back of the book.

Also by Gill Harvey

Egyptian Chronicles series
The Spitting Cobra
The Horned Viper
The Sacred Scarab

Also available
Orphan of the Sun

EGYPTIAN CHRONICLES

THE DEATH STALKER

GILL HARVEY

BLOOMSBURY

LONDON BERLIN NEW YORK

Bloomsbury Publishing, London, Berlin and New York

First published in Great Britain in April 2010 by Bloomsbury Publishing Plc
36 Soho Square, London, W1D 3QY

Text copyright © Gill Harvey 2010
Illustrations copyright © Peter Bailey 2010
The moral right of the author and illustrator has been asserted

A CIP catalogue record of this book is available from the British Library

ISBN 978 0 7475 9566 3

FSC
Mixed Sources
Product group from well-managed
forests and other controlled sources

Cert no. SGS - COC - 2061
www.fsc.org
© 1996 Forest Stewardship Council

Typeset by Dorchester Typesetting Group Ltd
Printed in Great Britain by Clays Ltd, St Ives plc, Bungay, Suffolk

1 3 5 7 9 10 8 6 4 2

www.bloomsbury.com/childrens
www.bloomsbury.com/gillharvey

For Diallo

CONTENTS

PROLOGUE

The wind whipped under the goatskin tent, gusting the sand inside. A girl lay there, curled up on a mat. She wiped a hand over her face groggily. There was sand everywhere. Sand in her ears. Sand on her eyelashes. Even sand in her mouth, and her skin was covered with a fine, gritty layer of it. The sandstorm had been blasting for hours.

Now, at last, it was blowing itself out. A young man entered the tent holding a bowl, and shook the girl's shoulder.

'Neith, it's time to get up,' he said. 'We must keep moving. The others are packing their tents.'

Neith barely stirred. 'Is there anything to eat?' she asked weakly.

'There is a little goat's milk. It will help with your thirst, too.' The man crouched down beside Neith and

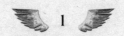 1

lifted her head. 'Here.' He tipped the bowl to her mouth.

The milk was warm and rich, and Neith gulped it gratefully.

'I'm sorry, Neith, that's all there is,' said her brother. 'But just think. We shall soon be there, and in Egypt there is plenty of everything.'

'Tell me about it again,' whispered Neith. 'Tell me, to give me strength.'

The young man stared out of the tent towards the horizon. 'They say there is a great river there,' he said. 'A great, beautiful river lined with trees. There are fruits in abundance – melons and grapes and figs. And there is sweet honey, the sweetest and finest in the world.' He stopped as his voice began to break.

'Go on,' Neith whispered.

'The river is full of fish, and the air full of birds . . . the gardens are lush, and the fields are wealthy with crops. Everyone wears elegant clothes and jewels, and their houses are full of the most exquisite crafts . . .'

'Hurry!' cried a voice outside.

Neith gazed up at her brother. 'Can it be true? Surely such a land does not exist.'

He stroked her hair. 'It is what they say, Neith. Come now. We must go.'

Neith struggled to her feet and helped her brother

to dismantle the goatskin shelter. The desert air was still full of sand, so that the line between land and sky was blurred. But as Neith slowly rolled up her mat, it seemed that the line was thicker, out towards the east.

'What's that?' she asked, pointing.

Her brother looked up from folding the goatskin covers. Together, they stared at the dense cloud of sand. It was getting bigger. Then, suddenly, it became clear what it was.

'Chariots! Soldiers! It's the Egyptian army!'

Neith's brother raised the alarm, and all the men rushed for their weapons, fumbling among their belongings in haste. The army drew closer, and Neith's heart quaked with fear. The Egyptian chariots were pulled by mighty horses; the feet of the soldiers beat a solid tattoo on the parched ground. Her companions were outnumbered two to one – they stood no chance at all.

'Let them show mercy . . .' she muttered under her breath.

The attackers' war cry chilled her blood. The chariots were charging. Sunlight flashed on bronze axes and daggers. Arrows flew, and Neith saw a friend of her brother's fall, pierced through the thigh. She watched in terror as her brother bounded forward, slashing an Egyptian with his dagger. The man fell and was trapped beneath the wheels of a chariot.

Neith gave a little cry. Her brother was fighting on, his dagger flailing wildly . . . she could no longer bear to watch. She sank to her knees and buried her face in her hands. They had come so far in the hope of reaching Egypt. Was it really going to end like this?

The men's battle raged. And then a cry rose up above the clash of swords.

'We must surrender!' called her brother. 'Or we shall surely die!'

The Egyptians were rampaging through the encampment. Neith looked up in time to see a soldier approaching her. She was yanked to her feet and dragged towards the other women, who screamed and wailed in terror.

Tears streaming down her cheeks, Neith scanned the camp for her brother. The men's hands were being tied behind their backs, and she just glimpsed him, shouting at his captors. One of them slapped him and she flinched, then bowed her head in grief. In all his tales of Egypt, her brother had never mentioned the army, or the possibility of capture. She had always imagined that they would arrive free and happy, as welcome arrivals in a plentiful land. Instead, they were prisoners of war.

CHAPTER ONE

It was Isis who heard them first.

'Listen!' she said, grabbing Mut's arm.

The two girls sat still as the noise grew closer. Hoof beats and rhythmic tramping, then the blast of a trumpet.

Isis scrambled to her feet. 'Come on!'

'We can't,' protested Mut. 'We have to wait for Mother's washing . . .'

But Isis was already running away from the river-bank and up the street. 'We'll come back afterwards!' she shouted over her shoulder.

She ran on into the town, where the commotion was getting louder. Mut caught up with her and they joined hands, weaving in and out of the crowds that were beginning to gather.

'Is it the king?' called a woman from a doorway.

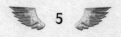

'No, no,' a man called back. 'It's the army! They're celebrating a victory!'

'Victory! Victory!'

The cry went up along the streets, and Isis felt her pulse quicken with excitement.

She and Mut made their way to the temple that dominated the centre of Waset. Both of them were dancers, small and supple, so it was easy to duck and wriggle their way through the milling people. Isis caught sight of chariot wheels, then peered around a man's shoulder to see ostrich plumes bobbing on horses' heads.

'Nearly there,' she said to Mut, and they dived forward one last time.

The rich, tangy smells of leather and sweat hit her nostrils as they emerged from the edge of the crowd. A row of five chariots clattered towards them, the horses prancing and tossing their heads, the drivers' arms bulging with muscles as they tugged on the reins. Behind each chariot driver stood a proud soldier waving a spear or a bow, encouraging the throng to cheer them on.

One chariot rode slightly in front of the others, and Isis noticed that its soldier was the only one wearing armour. 'We are the fighters of Amun!' he cried. 'He has given us victory again! Praise Amun,

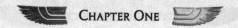

people of Waset!'

'Glory to Amun!' roared the crowd.

The chariots passed by, and behind them came a platoon of infantry – five rows of ten men marching in perfect time, each with a spear in one hand and a shield in the other. Isis saw that some of them had raw-looking cuts on their arms and chests, but they showed no pain on their faces.

'They're so brave,' she whispered in Mut's ear.

Mut nodded, her eyes wide with admiration.

The company had come to a halt, and up ahead, the leader was making an announcement.

'What's he saying?' Mut demanded of no one in particular.

The news filtered along the crowd. 'They've set up camp on the outskirts of Waset,' someone told them. 'They found Libyan marauders in the desert and defeated them, so they have come to give thanks at the temples here.'

Mut gripped Isis's hand more tightly. 'Did you hear that? They're camping here. You know what that means!'

Isis was puzzled. 'What?'

'They'll be looking for entertainment,' said Mut. 'We must tell Father. He could ask if they'd like to see the troupe. Wouldn't it be wonderful to perform for them?'

'Oh *yes*.' Isis grinned. It was a brilliant idea. 'Let's go and find him right now!'

Hopi heard the troops from further away – a drifting cacophony from the direction of the river as he and his tutor Menna prepared to go out on a visit.

Menna smiled. 'They like nothing better than the adulation of the crowds,' he commented. 'And why not? They have earned it.'

'Who are they?' asked Hopi.

'I heard that it is a company of the division of Amun,' said Menna. 'Just five platoons.' He grasped his walking stick. 'Come.'

Hopi followed Menna along the winding streets, listening to the distant noises. Menna was old and could not walk fast, but somehow the thought of fit, marching soldiers made Hopi all the more conscious of his own limp. It had been over five years since the jaws of a crocodile had inflicted his wounds, and they had healed as well as they ever would. He was lucky to be alive at all, but when he thought of able-bodied men and boys, he felt a pang of envy all the same.

Menna stopped at the door of one of the larger town houses, and knocked.

'My old friend Anty lives here,' he said. 'He is a

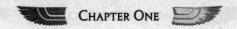

wise and well-respected scribe. He has summoned me – to celebrate the return of his son, no doubt.'

Hopi was surprised. He had imagined they were on a mission to treat someone for a snake bite or scorpion sting – that was what they usually did. But now, a servant opened the door and Menna entered. Hopi stepped in after him, noticing at once that this was the house of a wealthy man. It was lofty and spacious; fine murals were painted on the walls, while beautiful carvings and furniture were dotted about the rooms. A middle-aged man appeared from one of them and extended his arms in greeting.

'Menna, may the gods be with you. Life, prosperity, health!' he exclaimed. 'You have not come a moment too soon.'

'Anty.' Menna accepted the man's embrace, then stood back and surveyed his friend's worried expression. 'I had expected a celebration. Is something wrong?'

The scribe wrung his hands. 'I fear so, I fear so. Djeri has returned, sure enough. But he is wounded, Menna. They have brought him here.'

Menna seemed startled. 'He is not with his platoon?'

'No, no. That is why I called for you. Come.'

The two men hurried through the house, still talking.

'But I am not a doctor, Anty,' Menna was protesting.

'I know that, old friend, I know that.' Anty placed a hand on Menna's shoulder. 'The doctors have already been. But you have skills, nonetheless, you have powers, you are a priest . . .'

They entered a cool, dim room at the back of the house. A young man lay there, his eyes closed. Hopi stared. There was a deep gash on the man's shoulder, surrounded by red, swollen flesh. And that was not all. Hopi's eyes travelled down his body to the linen sheet that was draped over his legs. One of them bulged with bandages, but in spite of all the coverings, there was still blood and pus seeping through. Hopi didn't need to see any more to know that these were no minor wounds. This was serious. He was looking at a soldier who was very badly injured.

The company of troops was on the march again. After the first platoon of Egyptian soldiers, there was a platoon of Nubians, all carrying bows with a sheaf of arrows fastened around their waists. Isis found it difficult to tear her eyes away, but she knew they should go and fetch Paneb.

'They'll be marching up to the temples of Ipet-Isut,' she said. 'That's where they'll make their offerings.'

'So Father could try to talk to them on their way back,' agreed Mut. 'Come on, let's go.'

The two girls wove back through the crowds of people, then broke into a run and made for home. Mut's mother, Nefert, was tuning her lute in the courtyard.

'You two are home early!' she commented. 'Where's my washing? Is it finished?'

'We had to come home,' Mut explained breathlessly. 'There's a big group of soldiers in town. Father must speak to them –'.

'Soldiers?' Nefert's sister, Sheri, appeared at the courtyard door. 'Where?'

'They're camping just outside town,' said Isis. 'They've won a great victory and so they're here to give thanks to Amun. We *can* go and perform for them, can't we?'

'I don't know about that,' replied Nefert. Isis saw her throw a swift glance at Sheri.

'I'm going to tell Father,' insisted Mut. 'Where is he? Upstairs?'

'Wait –' began Nefert, but Mut was already scampering up the steps.

Isis hesitated, then followed her. 'I'm not sure Nefert wants to perform for the army,' she whispered as they reached the roof.

Mut pulled a face. 'Why ever not? Since all the harvest parties, we've hardly done a thing. We need the work.' She skipped up to her father, Paneb, who was studying a sheet of papyrus in the sun.

'Did I hear you mention work?' he asked, smiling at them.

Mut nodded and poured out the story of the soldiers. 'They'll be coming back through the town soon,' she finished. 'You will go and speak to them, won't you?'

Paneb looked thoughtful. 'Soldiers . . .' he murmured. 'Well, that is certainly worth thinking about. Leave it with me.'

'But you must come *now*!' protested Mut.

'All in good time,' said Paneb. 'As I said, leave it with me.'

Isis felt a little flat. She had been sure that Paneb would rush down to find the soldiers with them. 'We'd better go and get the washing,' she said to Mut.

Mut nodded glumly, and they headed out on to the street once more. The company had moved on now, along the great avenue that led to Ipet-Isut. The two girls made their way back to the place on the riverbank where the laundrymen laboured over their piles of linen.

'Thought we'd lost you!' joked one of the men on seeing Isis and Mut. He pointed at the flat stones where a row of garments was spread out in the sun. 'Yours are almost dry.'

Isis squatted down and watched as the men began sprinkling a fresh batch of wet linen with natron salt.

'I thought Paneb would jump at the idea,' she said.

Mut sat down next to her and sighed. 'It's probably because of Sheri and Kia.'

Isis was puzzled. 'Why because of them?'

'Their husbands.'

Isis was still lost. 'But neither of them has a husband.'

'They don't *now*, silly,' said Mut. 'But they did. They're widows. Their husbands were soldiers. Didn't you know?'

It was news to Isis, but then there were still many things that she didn't know about Mut's family. She and her brother, Hopi, had lived with them for less than a year. 'So what happened to them? Were they killed?'

Mut shrugged. 'Maybe.'

'In a battle?' Isis felt awed.

'I don't know. I've never heard them talk about it.'

The girls lapsed into silence. Isis watched one of the laundrymen *slap-slap* the linen on the rocks to pummel it clean. Another began to fold Nefert's linen into a neat stack. He divided it into two lots, then each girl balanced a pile on her head to take it home. As they dawdled along in the afternoon sun, Isis listened out for the sound of the soldiers returning, but all was quiet for the time being.

They turned into their own street. Suddenly, Mut leaped forward, almost dropping her load of linen.

'Father!'

Paneb was walking towards them, wearing his best linen kilt.

'Are you going to ask the soldiers after all?' demanded Mut.

Her father smiled. 'Yes. I have discussed it with the rest of the family. We've decided that it may be a good way to make a little extra grain now that the harvest is over.'

Isis felt a thrill of excitement. 'Can we come with you?' she asked.

Paneb looked at the two girls. 'I don't see why not. If anything is going to convince them to employ us, I'm sure you two will!'

The soldier's eyes flickered open. Hopi watched as he took in the faces gathered around him.

'Father,' he murmured.

'I am here, Djeri, my son,' said Anty. 'I have

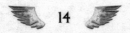

brought Menna to see you.'

Djeri nodded, then grimaced with pain and closed his eyes again.

'I must show Menna your injuries,' said Anty. 'I know the doctors have already examined you, but Menna has different skills. There may be other treatments that can help you.'

The soldier nodded and levered himself upwards. 'I will bear it as best I can.'

Menna hesitated, then stepped forward and lifted the sheet that covered Djeri's legs to reveal swathes of bloody bandages. Hopi tried to stifle a gasp. The pattern of the bloodstains was horribly familiar: it reminded him of how his own leg had looked, all those years ago.

'What happened?' Hopi blurted out. He knew that, as Menna's apprentice, it was not his place to speak, but he couldn't help himself.

Djeri's eyes swivelled around to meet his. He licked his dry, cracked lips. 'Who are you?' he asked. 'And why do you ask?'

Hopi flushed. 'I am Menna's apprentice,' he replied. 'And I ask because I bear similar wounds myself. They were inflicted in the river, by a crocodile.'

Djeri seemed interested. 'Well, you look alive to me,' he said. 'That's something. But my injuries are actually rather different. One of those desert barbarians struck me from my chariot –' his left hand drifted up towards the deep gash in his shoulder '– and I fell to the ground. It was the wheels of the chariots behind . . . behind me . . .' He paused, gulping, sweat breaking out on his brow. Slowly, carefully, Menna was unwrapping the bandages, and Hopi knew only too well that the pain must be excruciating. '. . . That . . . that gouged these wounds,' Djeri managed to finish.

He fell silent as Menna teased the linen free. It was encrusted with yellow pus as well as blood, which had stuck the fabric to the skin.

'They should have used more oils,' Menna muttered. He pulled at one of the bandages. 'I am sorry about this, Djeri.'

Djeri closed his eyes again, his forehead creased and his breathing shallow. Hopi could see that the pain was intense. In solidarity, he placed a hand on the soldier's good shoulder.

'He will, of course, receive great honour for his bravery,' said Anty. 'We expect the commander of the company to visit very soon.'

Menna had finished unwrapping the wounds and was gazing at them, deep in thought. They were a gruesome sight and they smelled bad, too.

'Is there anything you can do?' Anty asked him. 'He will live, will he not?'

'My brother, life or death rests in the hands of the gods. You know that.' Menna replied. 'I would have expected better of the army doctors, but I will do all I can. I must return home to fetch some supplies. Leave the bandages unwrapped for now.'

'Thank you. Thank you.' Anty bowed his head. 'We will do anything you say.'

'Then it is time to go.' Menna nodded to Hopi. 'Come, Hopi, we must be on our way.'

Isis and Mut danced around Paneb as they walked to the outskirts of Waset and beyond, into the desert, where the army had set up camp. Smoke from cooking fires rose into the air between the roughly constructed tents. With most of the soldiers in the town, it seemed quite deserted, so Isis thought they would be able to walk straight in. She soon realised she was mistaken. Hidden behind boulders were lookouts, heavily armed with bows and spears. One of them stepped out as they approached.

'Halt!' he cried. 'What is your business here?'

'We are performers,' Paneb told him. 'We have come to see whether the company requires entertainment.'

'Entertainment!' The soldier grinned. 'We've

plenty of prisoners of war to entertain us.'

'With respect, I imagine your commander seeks better entertainment than that,' said Paneb. 'We are one of the most sophisticated music and dance troupes in Waset.'

'Maybe. Anyway, I can't let you in,' said the lookout. 'You'll have to wait here.'

Paneb shrugged. 'Very well.'

They wandered over to a scrubby acacia tree to sit in the shade, and watched as the lookout disappeared behind his boulder once more. A breeze lifted the dusty sand, whirling it in eddies around them. The shadow of the tree grew longer.

'I can hear them,' announced Mut at last.

Isis listened. From the direction of Ipet-Isut came the faint *thump-thump, thump-thump* of soldiers' feet. 'Yes, I can, too,' she said.

They waited as the rhythmic thuds grew closer. There was something about them that made Isis quiver, but not with fear, exactly; it was more a sense of awe at something powerful, something much bigger than her – the might of Egypt itself.

The soldiers came into view, tramping out of the town in the same formation as before, a row of chariots riding before each infantry platoon. Isis noticed how each man stared straight ahead of him while keeping perfect time with the others. And now she could see that the company was bigger than she'd thought. After the first two platoons came two more, then about a hundred prisoners of war, with a final platoon bringing up the rear.

All the prisoners had their hands tied behind their backs. They looked miserable and exhausted. Isis stared at them, taking in their strange, colourful clothing and dark beards.

'Don't Libyans ever shave?' gasped Mut. No Egyptian man would go around looking like that.

'They live in the Red Land, the land of Seth,' said Paneb. 'It's no wonder they look so disorderly.' He took the two girls by the hand, one on either side of him. 'Come. Now is our chance to speak to the commander.'

As Paneb hurried them forward to the front of the company, Isis looked back, fascinated by the prisoners. Many of them were men, but there were some women, too, with long, bedraggled hair, and in the middle of the group were a few girls.

One of the girls caught her eye. She had a thin, narrow face that looked pinched with unhappiness. She noticed Isis staring at her, and her expression changed. Instead of misery, Isis saw a flare of anger and shame.

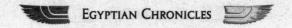

'Hurry up, Isis,' Paneb chided her.

Isis broke into a jog to match Paneb's stride, but couldn't resist one last glance. The girl's gaze was still fixed on her, but now she was begging, pleading with soulful eyes. Reluctantly, Isis turned away and looked ahead at the row of charioteers. But it felt as though the girl's eyes still followed her long after she had moved on, out of sight.

CHAPTER TWO

'I can't believe that a soldier of our own army has been treated so badly,' said Menna, rummaging through one of his caskets. 'The military doctors are supposed to be the best. Yet here am I, a priest of Serqet, trying to find medicines from my own supplies. They are all for bites and stings! I can't treat wounds like these . . .'

'But why?' asked Hopi. 'Why haven't they treated him better?'

Menna paused, his gnarled hands resting on an ointment bottle. 'There could be any number of reasons,' he reflected. 'War is brutal. The doctors have to prioritise.'

'You mean . . .' Hopi was struggling to take it all in. 'You mean, they didn't bother? They thought he would die anyway?'

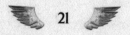

Menna's kind, wise eyes met his. 'Well, you saw his injuries.'

Now Hopi was horrified. 'Yes, but mine were just as awful, and I lived!'

The old priest smiled sadly. 'You were not at war,' he said, and turned back to the caskets.

Hopi was thinking hard, casting his mind back five years to the days when he, too, had been forced to lie still and entrust his life to doctors. He had been only eight, but he could still remember some of the details.

'Menna, let me go to the market,' he said. 'The wounds on my leg had a great deal of badness in them. The doctors treated them with fresh honey and castor oil – and I recovered. Perhaps these are what Djeri needs now.'

Menna stopped rummaging, his expression thoughtful. 'Perhaps you're right,' he said. 'I was looking for some malachite powder, but the wounds are probably too rotten for that. It's worth a try. Here, take some beads to barter with.'

Hopi accepted the beads and set off towards the riverbank, where the last traders would soon be packing up for the day. He felt pleased and honoured that Menna had agreed with his ideas, and felt doubly gratified that it was he who could offer some help to Djeri. The soldier's fate had affected him deeply – it had brought back many memories. His own recovery had been terribly slow and painful, but it had also changed his life. As he had healed, the gods had seemed to touch him and call him to his vocation. It was strange that Djeri's wounds were so similar, superficially at least. Perhaps the gods had willed it that way.

Finding an oil vendor was easy enough, but it took a little longer to find the honey. At last, Hopi came across an old woman sitting on her own, with just a big pot in front of her. In its depths, Hopi spotted fresh honeycomb.

'The blessing of Sekhmet be upon you,' she said, as Hopi traded the beads.

'Why do you say that?' Hopi asked fearfully. 'She is the goddess of war.'

'But also of healing,' the old woman replied. 'I sense her presence around you.'

A little mystified, Hopi hurried back to Menna. Without further ado, they returned to the house of Anty, where the servant let them in.

The soldier was feverish. His body was clammy, his cheeks burned to the touch, and this time he did not open his eyes and speak to them.

'He is worse,' muttered Anty. 'He is drawing close to the Next World.'

'He is in the hands of the gods, brother,' said Menna.

'Only they know the direction in which he is travelling.'

Hopi brought out the pots of oil and honey that he had bought, and together he and Menna set about re-inspecting the wounds.

'Brother, I must be honest with you,' Menna said to Anty. 'I don't know the right spells to speak over wounds such as these. We will have to trust that this treatment will be enough.'

'It comes with the blessing of Sekhmet,' said Hopi. He felt surprisingly calm. 'Menna, will you allow me to dress the wounds? They must be cleaned first.'

The old man nodded. 'Of course, Hopi. Your hands are surer than mine.'

Hopi moistened a soft linen cloth in a bowl of water and began the delicate job of wiping away the worst of the pus. Djeri cried out and tossed in pain on the bed. Hopi dampened the cloth again and laid it on the wounds for a moment, soothing them.

'This apprentice seems old for his years,' commented Anty in surprise.

Menna nodded. 'Those who have suffered are always the ones with greatest wisdom,' he said.

Hopi felt a warm glow at Menna's words. Gradually, the old man was allowing him to treat more and more of the patients who came to them. Hopi had learned most of the remedies for both snake bites and scorpion stings; only a few of the most difficult remained, and that was because they required a powerful level of magic. Menna had even started to pay him regularly, which he knew was a sure sign of the old man's trust.

He worked quickly and quietly while Menna and Anty looked on. When he had finished, he put the bowl to one side.

'I have something to ask of you,' he said to Anty.

'Please ask,' Anty replied.

'Allow me to stay with him,' said Hopi. 'I would like to see how he is, later on.'

'Why, yes, of course you may. I would be very grateful,' said Anty. 'But don't you have a family of your own to go to?'

'They will understand,' said Hopi. 'Perhaps you could send a message, Menna? Isis will want to know where I am.'

In the last light of dusk, Ramose was chasing his younger brother Kha around the rooftop, bellowing and waving a stick. The rest of the family sat around and relaxed; Isis and Mut were playing a game of *senet* in one corner.

'Kha's a Libyan!' he shouted. 'I'm going to chop his head off!'

Kha shrieked in mock terror, then crashed into the wall and collapsed in a heap. Ramose pounced on him and put the stick to his throat.

'Surrender or die,' he growled.

'Surrender!' Kha squeaked, then rolled over and jumped to his feet again.

'Careful!' cried Mut, as Kha catapulted towards her.

Sheri looked up from gently plucking her lyre. 'Yes, that's enough, you two,' she told the boys. 'You'll end up hurting someone.'

Ramose threw the stick down and flopped on to a mat next to his father. 'I want to come and see the soldiers,' he said, with a pout. 'Everyone else is going and we have to stay here.'

'Don't be silly, Ramose.' Nefert's voice was firm. 'We're only going because we have to.'

'When I grow up, I want to be a soldier,' said Ramose. 'I want to go to war.'

Paneb chuckled and tugged playfully on his son's side-lock.

'Don't encourage him.' Nefert's voice was sharp. 'You would not wish such a fate for him.'

A heavy silence fell upon the adults. Isis and Mut exchanged glances. Since their return from the army camp, the atmosphere in the house had been strange. On hearing that Paneb had managed to arrange a performance, the women had said very little. They had pursed their lips and nodded, then they had got on with their chores. A new job usually meant lots of questions and a long discussion about the performance. But not this time.

'Your move,' said Mut.

Isis realised she wasn't concentrating on the game. She hurriedly moved a piece, then returned to her thoughts. She wanted to ask Sheri and Kia about their husbands. She wanted to speak to Hopi about going to the army camp, but her brother was out for the night. Above all, she wished she could forget the face of the Libyan girl that she had seen among the prisoners of war, but those deep, dark eyes would not go away. Who was she? Isis wondered. Could she speak any Egyptian? There was a whole night and day to wait until they went back to the camp. Then, maybe, she would see the girl again.

I'll go and look for her, Isis told herself. *I'm sure I'll be able to find her*.

'Your move again,' said Mut. 'Where on earth are you, Isis?'

Once Menna had left, a servant brought oil lamps to light the darkening room, and Anty fetched Hopi some bread and beer. Djeri had still not opened his eyes. The moments passed slowly. Anty came in and out, fretting over his son, then at last left Hopi alone. Hopi kept a watchful eye on Djeri, looking for any sign of change.

At last, he stirred and groaned. 'Father,' he muttered.

'He's not here at the moment. I am caring for you,' Hopi told him.

Djeri opened his eyes a fraction. He frowned, struggling to recollect. 'You . . . you are . . .'

'Hopi. Menna's apprentice.' Hopi reached for a beaker of beer. 'Try to drink. This is good beer. It will nourish you.' He tipped a little into the side of the soldier's mouth.

Djeri swallowed, choked and coughed. But most of the beer went down the right way.

'Thank you.' Djeri closed his eyes again, but he did not sleep. 'All I can feel is pain,' he whispered. 'It's like a tomb . . . a dark place from which there is no escape . . .'

'I know,' said Hopi quietly. 'I have been there, too.'

He carried on giving Djeri mouthfuls of the rich beer, waiting each time to check that the soldier was ready for more. Djeri gulped and gasped, as though even drinking was exhausting him. Then, outside the room, they heard voices.

'He's in here, sir,' Hopi heard Anty say, as Djeri's

father hurried in, followed by a tall, imposing man in leather armour. His muscular, broad-shouldered body threw a wide shadow on to the wall; he seemed too big for the room.

Djeri's eyes fluttered open. A look of shock spread over his face. 'Commander,' he managed to say.

The man strode to Djeri's side. 'You are still alive, then,' he commented.

'Yes, sir.' Djeri's voice was faint.

The commander cast a glance at Djeri's body, his eyes roving over his wounded leg.

'If I may get you something, sir –' began Anty.

'No, no.' The commander waved him away. 'You know why I am here, Djeri. You have brought great honour to your platoon.'

'Thank you, sir,' said Djeri weakly. 'I only did my duty to our god the king.'

The commander nodded. 'And the king rewards those who serve him loyally.'

He snapped his fingers towards the door. A guard stepped into the room and handed him a wooden box. The commander raised the lid and lifted out a necklace. Hopi stared at it. Dangling at the bottom, threaded between beads of jasper and turquoise, was a little fly made out of pure gold, glinting in the light of the oil lamps.

'Djeri, son of Anty,' said the commander. 'I confer upon you the Order of the Golden Fly.' And he laid the necklace across Djeri's chest.

The soldier's fingers groped feebly for the fly. 'Thank you, commander,' he said. 'I hope I shall soon return to duty.'

The commander gave no reply. He stood at the foot of the bed for a moment, then turned and swept out of the room with his guard at his heels. Anty hurried after them to let them out.

Hopi sat still. He could not take his eyes off the golden fly that now lay across the covers. Djeri must have been a true warrior on the battlefield. What an honour! All the same, it seemed strange that there had been so little ceremony, so little fuss. He thought the commander could have waited until Djeri was with his platoon.

And then it occurred to him – Djeri was lucky to be alive. As far as the army doctors were concerned, he was probably dead already. He may never return to his platoon, for even if he survived, he would never be strong enough to stand and fight in a chariot. He would become a cripple, like Hopi. But Djeri was clearly unaware of that. He had talked of returning to duty. And who would be the person to tell him that he would never fight again?

Isis watched as Hopi mechanically lifted some bread to his mouth. He looked drained, as though he had hardly slept. He had shown up just as the family were eating breakfast in the courtyard.

'It's not like Menna to keep you out all night,' said Sheri, handing him a beaker of beer. 'Was it a bite or a scorpion sting?'

Hopi shook his head. 'Neither.' He took a swig of the beer. 'It was an injured soldier. Djeri, son of Anty. A company from the division of Amun is camped outside the –'

'We know that.' Mut cut Hopi short. 'We're going to perform for them this evening.'

'Really? You're going to the camp?' Hopi looked around at everyone in surprise.

Isis nodded. 'They've taken us on for three evenings. We saw them march through town, on their way to give thanks at the temples.'

'Well, it was an important victory. I expect they made a lot of offerings,' said Hopi. He reached for another piece of bread. 'Djeri received a great honour last night, from the commander himself. He was given the Order of the Golden Fly.'

Isis noticed that suddenly, the women were listening intently.

'What does that mean?' asked Mut.

'It's a kind of award,' said Hopi. 'He was given a necklace with a fly made of gold strung on it.'

'Who is this man?' demanded Kia.

'Djeri? He's a charioteer.'

'An officer, or one of the rank and file?' Now Kia's voice was sharp and her eyes were flashing. Isis looked at her in astonishment. Why should Hopi's news make her angry? Hopi seemed equally taken aback.

'I don't know,' he said. 'Not all the charioteers are officers, I don't think.'

'So what did he do to receive this great honour?'

'He fought bravely,' said Hopi. 'He was part of an attack against the Libyans and he was knocked from his chariot.'

'So he was doing his job, and for this he has been richly rewarded.' Kia's voice seemed to become ever more bitter.

Isis felt the tension rising in the courtyard. Hopi seemed nonplussed. He didn't reply for a moment, but took in the expectant faces around him.

'Well,' he said at last, 'he may have been rewarded, but he may also lose his life.'

'Such is the soldier's lot,' said Sheri softly. 'To fight, to die for Egypt. We knew that, Kia, did we not?'

'We *know* very little,' retorted Kia.

'And now is our chance to find out more.' Sheri placed a hand on Kia's arm.

Kia pulled her arm away. 'No, Sheri. It is too late for that.'

'It is never too late, sister. We could talk to them. The company is here, on our doorstep. We are even going to visit them. We can find out –'

'No!' Kia almost shouted. Her chest was heaving. 'No, sister. It is too long ago. The lives of soldiers are short. It may be the same company, but it will not be the same men. Any inquiry is bound to fail. My suffering is buried deep inside me. I cannot bear to unearth it again now.'

The sisters stared at each other. Nefert leaned forward and placed a comforting arm around each of them.

'As you wish, sister,' said Sheri eventually, her voice soft and sad. 'I would not wish to do anything that might cause you further pain.'

CHAPTER THREE

Paneb and Nefert led the way out to the fringes of the desert. Isis was feeling nervous, but she wasn't sure why. Of course she was always a little bit nervous before performing, but this was different. She had never been inside an army camp before. As they approached, a shiver ran down her spine. Guards loomed up holding flaming torches, and escorted them past rows of simple tents stretching out into the darkness. Isis glimpsed shields and daggers propped up against the tents, and saw a group of dozing horses tethered near a row of chariots. Then she peered into the gloom, wondering where the prisoners were kept. She could see no sign of them.

The troupe was taken to the centre of the camp. Here, the atmosphere was livelier, with soldiers laughing and joking around a wide open area. It was circular, a kind of arena, lit by a larger fire and more guards holding torches. At one end, seated on an elegant wooden chair, sat the man who had led the company through Waset, Commander Meref. A fan-bearer stood behind his shoulder and officers at either side. He got to his feet as the troupe walked towards him.

'Ah, the entertainers!' Meref beckoned them. 'Let us see what you're made of before the wrestling begins.'

Wrestling! So *that* was what the arena was for. Isis sized up the soldiers gathering to watch. Their faces were young, but they seemed hardened, their eyes glittering in the leaping light of the fire and the torches. She stood close to Mut, holding her hand as they waited for the musicians to get ready.

Nefert began plucking her lute. Sheri and Kia joined in on the lyre and the flute, while Paneb kept time with the clappers. Isis and Mut began to dance, bowing and swaying, then moving on to energetic somersaults and pirouettes. The soldiers applauded and cheered, their voices raucous, and Isis tried not to hear what they were saying. Some of the men were rude.

The first routine over, the women laid down their instruments while Isis and Mut slipped into the shadows. They found a place near the commander's chair to see what would happen next. The atmosphere around the arena was building, and the men started calling out names.

'Bring on Nes, the Lion!' some cried.

'No, no! Let us see Mose, the Great Bull!'

Then there was a loud cheer as the first two wrestlers stepped into the arena wearing nothing but rough linen loincloths, their bodies shining with oil. They prowled around, waiting for the right moment, and then one of them pounced. The two men clung on to each other, breathing hard, both trying to get a grip on the other's slippery skin. The soldiers surrounding them took sides, urging on their comrades, until one of them rolled his opponent on to his back and pinned him to the ground in the dust.

The soldiers bellowed their approval, pumping their fists into the air. They were much more excited about the wrestling than they'd been about the music and dancing. The troupe was sidelined; it wasn't even clear if they would perform a second routine. Isis realised this was her chance to explore.

'I'm just going to the toilet,' she whispered to Mut.

Her dance partner's eyes were transfixed by the wrestlers. She didn't even seem to hear.

Isis slipped away from the crowded area and

melted into the darkness. Away from the arena, the night was quiet, the sky studded with stars. She could hear the sound of her own breathing, nervous and shallow. Isis surveyed the camp with its rows of tents, thinking that the prisoners must be somewhere close by. Keeping to the shadows, she made her way to the far end of the camp.

By the light of the moon, she spotted a row of stakes that formed a kind of enclosure. Guards were posted around it at regular intervals. Isis crept closer, then ducked behind a chariot and dropped down to lie on her belly. Now, she could just about see inside.

Peeping between the stakes, she saw people. The prisoners of war were there, huddled together on the bare sand. Isis took in their limp bodies and haggard faces. Their hands were no longer tied behind their backs, but Isis could see lengths of rope entwined around their ankles. It was a very different scene from the one she'd witnessed at the arena. Dragging herself a little closer, she peered beyond rows of men, looking for the women. And then a movement caught her eye.

Two of the prisoners were talking to each other. One was the girl she had seen before, sitting next to a young man. Isis shifted around beneath the chariot, trying to get a better view of their faces. She studied them, fascinated. In spite of the man's beard, it was easy to see that they were from the same family. Isis guessed that they were brother and sister.

The girl seemed very upset. She gripped the man's arm and shook her head. Isis thought that she could see the glimmer of tears on her cheeks. The man seemed to be remonstrating, trying to convince her of something. Then Isis saw what it was. The man put his hand to his ankle. The rope that encircled it looked secure enough but, with a deft movement, the man slipped it off his foot. He had managed to free himself.

Isis felt her heart beating faster. From her hiding place, she looked up and down the line of guards. There were two quite close by and it would be madness to try to get past them. Dangling from each of the guards' waists was a little trumpet – they could draw the attention of the whole company in no time. The young Libyan looked tired and weak. He couldn't run far, surely?

Minutes passed. Isis knew she must return to the arena before anyone noticed she was missing. She watched as the Libyan man cupped the girl's face in his hands. Now her tears were clear to see. He stroked her hair and placed a soft kiss on her forehead.

He's going for it, thought Isis, her mouth dry. *He's going to try to escape.*

A big roar went up from the direction of the arena. Isis felt a stab of anxiety. She must go back. She began to wriggle out, but took one last look at the pair before she left. The girl had bent her head and was quietly sobbing. Isis longed to help her, but what could she do? She pulled herself up from underneath the chariot and dusted herself down. Then, silently, she ran back to the rest of the troupe, hoping desperately that the Libyan would change his mind.

All was quiet, apart from the sound of Djeri's breathing. Hopi wiped the sweat from the soldier's forehead, terrified that he was slowly slipping away – away from this world, and into the next.

'You must fight,' he said urgently, close to the soldier's ear. 'You fought the Libyans. Now you must fight for your life. You must not give up, Djeri.'

For a second, Djeri's eyes flickered open.

Hopi shook his good shoulder gently. 'Can you hear me? Do you understand what I am saying?'

Djeri gave the tiniest nod of his head, and Hopi sighed in relief.

'You are good to me, Hopi,' the soldier said faintly, and closed his eyes again.

So he was still with them, just about. It was strange, how Hopi felt about this soldier. He admired his courage and bravery, but it was more than that. It was as though they had a connection, an understanding that could not be put into words. Their injuries were so alike, and even beyond that, Hopi felt something else. Something deeper. But he did not know what it was.

Then Djeri's lips moved. He began to speak, his voice barely above a whisper. 'Tell me . . .' he croaked. 'Tell me the truth.'

Hopi was puzzled. 'The truth about what?'

'I am not a fool,' muttered Djeri. 'Tell me what will happen, should I live.'

Hopi felt his pulse quicken. He licked his lips. 'You mean . . . your leg?' He looked at Djeri's bandages, tongue-tied.

'Will I be able to walk?'

So, that was it. Hopi took a deep breath and thought for a moment. Was it really up to him to break the news? It didn't seem fair. Then again, perhaps he was the best person; maybe the gods had sent him to help.

'I think . . . I think you will be like me,' he said eventually. 'My wounds were similar to yours.'

Djeri's eyes flew open. He had seen Hopi come and

go, of course; but suddenly, he looked at him properly, as though for the first time. With a huge effort, he
hoisted himself on to his elbow.

'Walk across the room,' he instructed, with sur-
prising strength in his voice.

Hopi's mouth dropped open. 'I don't –'

'Walk!' ordered Djeri.

Reluctantly, Hopi got up from the stool he was sitting on and stepped over to the doorway. He could
not hide his limp. There was no disguising the way
his right leg dragged with every step. He was
mortified. He turned and saw Djeri's expression. The
soldier's mouth was curled with anguish and disgust. Their eyes met, then Djeri's slid away, hard and
bitter.

'A cripple,' Hopi heard him mutter, as he flopped
back down on the bed to stare up at the ceiling.

Hopi's cheeks were burning with indignation. He
made his way back to the stool. 'It's not that bad! I
still get around and work. I'm not a cripp—' He
stopped abruptly. He knew that he *was* a cripple, as
far as a soldier was concerned.

But now Djeri seemed lost in his own world. His
breathing became shallow again, harsh gasps that
frightened Hopi.

'It is the punishment of the gods!' he burst out.

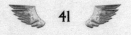

'No, no,' Hopi protested. 'Djeri, the injuries of a soldier bring only honour.'

Djeri's eyes focused on Hopi's face. 'Believe me, my friend,' he said. 'When I talk of punishment, I know what I am saying. There is sickness in this company of Amun. A great sickness that eats the souls of men.'

'What? What sickness?'

Djeri's words didn't make sense. *The fever has taken him*, thought Hopi desperately.

He reached for a beaker of wine.

'Djeri, drink this. It's the fever talking. You need to sleep.'

But in his anger, Djeri seemed to have found a new energy. He tried to sit up again, his eyes flaming and the veins sticking out in his neck. 'Don't speak to me of fever! I tell you, the gods have spoken!' he cried wildly. 'See what they have done to me!'

Hopi got to his feet and tried to push the soldier back down. 'Hush, hush,' he soothed him. 'Djeri, please lie down.'

The shouting brought people running. Anty rushed in, followed by two of his servants. 'What's going on here?' demanded the scribe. 'What's happening, my son?'

Djeri's eyes were bulging and there were flecks of

spit on his lips. 'We are doomed!' he cried. 'Ma'at is no longer with us. She will judge our hearts in the Next World and they will fail. We shall be devoured by Ammut. There will be no mercy . . . no mercy . . .' Djeri's voice grew weaker again, and he collapsed back down on the bed.

Anty looked stricken. 'He is elsewhere. Even now, he is not in this world.' He placed a hand on his son's forehead, then dropped to his knees at the bedside and clung on to Djeri's hands. 'Oh, my boy, my boy,' he groaned. 'Stay with us. Stay . . .' Tears dripped down his cheeks to land on his pale, clenched knuckles.

He stayed like that for some time, mouthing prayers to all the gods, while Djeri lay still and silent. At last, Anty rose and beckoned one of his servants.

'Send word to Djeri's brothers. They must come and pay their respects. Summon his younger sisters and their children. All must come soon, before it is too late.'

Hopi watched in anguish. He could not bring himself to tell the old scribe what had happened. But now that the room was quiet again, the soldier's breathing sounded easier. Looking at his face, Hopi knew that Djeri was not raving. He had been devastated at the news about his leg. And the rest – the talk of sickness and punishment? Was it delirium, madness? *No, it isn't that*, thought Hopi. In some way, he sensed that the soldier had been telling the truth.

The roar that Isis had heard was for the great wrestler Nes, the one the soldiers called the Lion. As Isis nudged up to Mut to watch, she soon worked out that he was pitted against his chief rival, the equally enormous Mose, the Great Bull. The soldiers watching were hollering the two men's names at full pitch. The noise was deafening. Perhaps, thought Isis hopefully, no one would hear if the prisoners' guards called the alarm . . .

The wrestlers circled one another, their eyes knowing and wary. Isis guessed they had fought each other many times before. And yet, she noticed, Nes the Lion was much older than his opponent. His muscles were gnarled and sinewy, like bunches of hemp rope, and the lines of his face were etched deeply. But there was no doubting his power.

It was Mose who made the first move, diving in to grasp Nes by the thigh. His hands lost their hold on the slippery oil and Nes spun round to free himself. Then he sidestepped and grabbed Mose by the arm, twisting it behind his back. Nes's supporters erupted in applause, but Mose wasn't trapped for long.

Jamming his knee between Nes's legs, he pushed him off balance and loosened his opponent's grip. Mose's supporters crowed.

Then, above the tumult of the contest, Isis heard the sound she was dreading: the high, tinny blast of a trumpet. She stared around at the soldiers.

Don't hear, don't hear, she willed them.

The wrestlers now had their arms locked around each other, pushing with all the strength of their massive shoulders. Isis held her breath.

It was no use. There it was again – the shrill, insistent summons, louder and more urgent this time. Nes heard it and raised his head. Isis looked at Commander Meref. He was listening, too.

At once, the wrestling bout broke up. A group of soldiers was sent running towards the prisoners' enclosure. Commander Meref barked some orders. The rest of the company shuffled into formation, each man in his own platoon, and stood to attention. In seconds, the atmosphere had changed. The arena was silent. Isis heard one of the horses snort nearby. The fire spat and crackled, but none of the soldiers moved.

Isis looked over to where Mut, Paneb, Nefert and her sisters were standing, their faces shocked and bewildered. Isis felt slightly sick. The tear-stained face of the Libyan girl swam into her mind. How right she had been to beg her brother not to be so foolish.

There were shouts in the distance. Isis heard a woman's cry. She imagined it might be the girl, calling out in despair. Then there was the sound of tramping feet and animated voices, and Isis saw a torch bobbing along, approaching the arena. Half of her wanted to look away, but the other half was compelled to watch as the soldiers appeared, dragging the prisoner of war between them. They reached the arena and stopped in front of Commander Meref.

One of the soldiers saluted. 'Trying to escape, sir. We caught him heading out to the desert.'

The young man looked up at the commander and poured out a stream of his own language. Isis could not understand a word, but she understood the feelings on his face – the anger, the defiance and the fear. The commander regarded him coldly.

'A pity,' he grunted. 'He is one of the stronger ones. But we must make an example of him, all the same.'

'Shall we beat him, sir?' asked the soldier. 'Or . . .' He seemed to hesitate. 'There is the –'

'I know what the options are,' thundered the commander. He rose to his feet, a thin smile playing on his lips. 'Keep close guard on him overnight. Tomorrow he will be sent to the pit.'

A murmur ran through the ranks of soldiers. Isis stared at the young man. It was clear that he had no idea what his fate would be, and for that matter neither did she. But from the soldiers' response, she could sense that it would be a terrible one.

The commander did not sit down again. The episode seemed to have dulled his appetite for entertainment. 'Everyone is dismissed,' he ordered. Then he turned to Paneb. 'And that, my man, includes you.'

For a second, no one moved, as though a spell had been cast on the gathering. Then the soldiers began to drag the prisoner away, kicking and screaming, and the platoon officers started to give orders. With a click of his fingers to the fan-bearer, Commander Meref strode off into the night.

CHAPTER FOUR

Djeri's eldest brother was the first to arrive at the house of Anty. He could not have looked more different to the soldier. Being the eldest, he had followed in his father's footsteps, and had the soft paunch and gentle hands of a scribe. Hopi retreated to the corner of the room and bowed his head as the firstborn kissed the forehead of his younger brother, but Djeri had fallen into a deep, troubled sleep.

It was not another family member who arrived next, but Menna, holding a torch. He put his head round the door.

'Hopi, come here,' he said, beckoning him out of the room.

Obediently, Hopi went to him.

'Anty tells me that Djeri has started to talk about the Next World,' said Menna in a low voice. 'He has

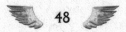

taken this as a sign that he will not remain with us much longer. What do you think?'

Hopi's feelings were in turmoil. 'I don't know,' he said. 'He is suffering greatly and the fever is upon him. But it's more than that, Menna. He got upset.' He hesitated, unsure how much to say. 'There is something on his mind. Something that must be resolved in this world, and not the next.'

Menna stroked his chin. 'Do you believe he will live until the morning?'

'Well, it's difficult to be sure. But I think so, yes.'

'Good. In that case you must leave and go to your own home. You may return tomorrow, but for now, the family must be allowed some time with Djeri. Having his family around him for a few hours will do no harm, and may indeed speed his healing.'

'Very well.' Hopi felt slightly relieved, for he was exhausted.

'You need to rest,' said Menna. 'But tomorrow I want you to come and talk to me. I want to hear what you think is plaguing the young man's mind. Now, let's go.'

They took their leave of Anty and headed into the night.

Back at home, Hopi was surprised to discover that the troupe had just returned and was sitting on the roof. It was not very late; usually their performances would keep them out for many hours, sometimes until dawn.

'Hopi!' Isis got up and hugged him as he appeared. 'I need to speak to you,' she whispered. 'Let's go downstairs.'

They took one of the little oil lamps and slipped away down to the courtyard.

'So what happened?' asked Hopi. 'Why are you back so early?'

Isis described the wrestling matches, and how they had been interrupted by the young Libyan trying to escape. 'I'm sure they're going to do something horrible to him – really horrible.'

Hopi sighed. 'They're prisoners of war, Isis. They are our enemies and are lucky to be alive at all.' Hopi was still reeling at what had happened with Djeri, and he didn't understand what all the fuss was about. To his astonishment, his sister's eyes filled with tears.

'But it's awful, Hopi! I saw a girl,' Isis gulped. 'I saw her yesterday and I haven't been able to stop thinking about her.'

'A girl? You mean, a Libyan girl?' Hopi was beginning to think that Isis had lost her senses.

She nodded, tears beginning to fall. 'Yes. And

tonight I sneaked away during the wrestling and saw the prisoners' enclosure. It was dreadful. I saw the same girl again. It was her brother who tried to escape, and now he's going to be punished.'

It was all too much for Hopi. He thought of Djeri lying in agony on his bed, and of his family gathered around him right now, paying their respects. He thought of Djeri's disgust at the idea of being a cripple, and felt a strange wave of shame and anger.

'She is nothing but a Libyan. Men have been killed to protect us from those people,' he said savagely. 'Her brother deserves everything he gets.'

Isis stopped crying. She looked up at him with tears still standing on her cheeks. 'Do you really think that?'

'Yes, Isis, I do.' Hopi lowered his voice. 'And you would be wise not to express these feelings about Libyans. People may think you are disloyal to the king – and the gods.' He took hold of her hands and squeezed them. 'Promise me you will not breathe a word to anyone else.'

Now Isis looked full of fear. 'I won't,' she promised. She searched his face, and Hopi knew that she would see the turmoil written there. 'Are *you* all right, Hopi? How's your soldier?'

Hopi hesitated. If there was anyone he could talk

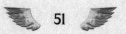

to, it was Isis. But somehow he still felt too confused and upset to tell her everything. 'He's struggling. His injuries . . . they're a bit like mine, Isis.'

'Oh, Hopi.' Isis hugged him. 'I'm sorry. That must be awful for you.'

'It's all right. I think he will live.'

'Are you going back to see him tomorrow?' asked Isis.

Hopi nodded. 'Yes.'

Isis picked at the wall of the courtyard, where a piece of plaster was flaking off. She seemed to be thinking something over. Then she looked at him. 'Could you ask him something for me?'

Hopi frowned. 'What sort of thing?'

Isis looked up at him with wide, serious eyes. 'Ask him what they do in the pit.'

'The pit? What's that?'

'If I knew, I wouldn't be asking,' said Isis. She hugged him again. 'So will you, or not?'

Hopi sighed and extricated himself gently. 'Yes, Isis. If you insist, I will.'

Back up on the roof, Isis lay on her mat and stared at the stars. The whole day had left her head whirling. She tossed and turned, trying to put the prisoners of war out of her mind. Could Hopi be right? Was it really disloyal to the king to worry about the happiness of Libyans? *She* knew she wasn't disloyal. She felt sorry for the girl, that was all. And now that she knew she had an older brother, she felt it all the more. Weren't all brothers and sisters the same? She heard a jackal call in the desert, and wondered if the Libyan girl was warm enough in that enclosure. She imagined her shivering, hungry and cold, her brother taken from her.

Sleep came at last. Isis woke early and went down to the courtyard to splash her face with water in the pale light of dawn. Sheri was awake, too, stoking the embers of the bread oven. Isis helped her, passing her little twigs at first, then larger ones as the flames began to grow. Sheri seemed tired and withdrawn, and Isis guessed that going to the army camp hadn't been easy for her.

'Sheri,' she said, 'what do you think happened to your husbands?'

Sheri turned her head quickly to stare at Isis. For a second, Isis thought she would not reply. Then she said sadly, 'We don't know what happened to either of them, Isis.'

'Why did nobody tell you?'

'We received a message that they were dead.' Sheri placed a little extra emphasis on the word *dead*, then turned back to the oven and began poking at the twigs.

'And they belonged to this company of Amun?' Isis persisted.

'Yes –' Sheri's voice broke a little, and she cleared her throat. 'Yes, they did.'

Isis fell silent, thinking it through. Surely there was someone who could give them information, if they asked. 'Did they know each other – your husband and Kia's?'

'They were friends. We met them at the same time, when we were girls.' The fire was now burning well, and Sheri stood up. She reached for a bowl of flour that had been covered overnight, and poured in some water to make a dough. 'I know you are curious, Isis, so I shall tell you the truth. Before we became musicians, Kia and I were dancers, like you and Mut. We performed for a platoon of soldiers and we were wooed by two of them. We married them, even though our parents were against the idea, and while the platoon was in Waset, we were happy. Then the men were summoned north, and that was it. We never saw them again.'

Isis listened as Sheri's long-fingered hands began to pummel the dough. The story filled her with sadness, and she didn't know what to say.

'We thought . . . we thought there might be some compensation,' Sheri carried on. 'We had heard that soldiers were rewarded well for their valour. Land, gold, slaves . . .' She shook her head. 'But we received nothing. And we heard nothing more. We returned here, to the house of our parents, and here we have remained. We are only grateful that Nefert found a good husband, to make up for our mistakes.' Sheri kept her head bent as she kneaded away. Then she looked at Isis and smiled. 'So let that be a lesson to you, Isis,' she said, and now her tone was playful. 'Be very careful who you choose to marry.'

Isis smiled back, relieved that Sheri could still be cheerful. 'I don't think I'll marry *anyone*,' she declared. 'Anyway, I won't just yet.' Then she had another thought. 'Sheri, did losing your husband make you hate the Libyans?'

Sheri looked startled. 'Hate them?' She thought for a moment. 'We don't know how our men died. It could have been at the hands of Hittites, or the Sea People, or any of Egypt's enemies. In any case, the army is full of foreigners. My husband would have had some as friends.'

'Really?' Isis was intrigued. 'So it's not wrong to care about them, is it?'

'You do ask some strange questions.'

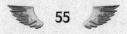

'But *is* it wrong?' Isis was desperate to know.

Sheri rubbed her cheek with a floury hand. 'Well, no, I don't suppose it is.'

When Hopi arrived at Anty's house, he found Djeri fast asleep. To Hopi's relief, the soldier's breathing was deeper, more regular, and his forehead was cool – the fever had subsided. He began the laborious job of undressing his wounds to check on their progress. As he began to unwrap the bandages, the soldier woke up.

'Argh, don't,' he muttered through gritted teeth.

'I have to. I'm sorry,' said Hopi. He surveyed his work from the day before. The wounds still had a long, long way to go before they would heal properly, but there was some improvement.

'Where is everyone?' demanded Djeri.

'Your family is in the courtyard,' said Hopi. 'Your father told me you're better, but I wanted to see it for myself.'

'Is that what I am? Better?' Djeri sounded unconvinced.

Hopi nodded. 'Yes. Your fever has gone.' He decided to say no more about the soldier's future. Instead, he remembered what Menna had said, about finding out what was on his mind. 'But last night you were very upset. You seemed convinced that the gods are punishing you.' He paused. 'No one else thinks this, Djeri.'

A frown appeared on the soldier's brow. 'They do not know what I know.' Djeri spoke clearly, quietly. He was certainly not raving now.

'Tell me,' prompted Hopi. 'It can't be that bad.'

But the soldier shook his head, mute.

Seconds passed as Hopi tried to think of a way forward. 'When the gods injured me, it wasn't a punishment,' he said eventually. 'It was then that they gave me my gift.'

'And what is that?'

'My understanding of feared creatures,' said Hopi. 'Snakes, scorpions, lizards and the great crocodiles that live in the Nile.'

For the first time, the hint of a smile appeared on Djeri's face. 'You believe that this was a gift?'

'Of course,' said Hopi.

Djeri's eyes met Hopi's. 'I, too, have a love of these creatures.'

Hopi stared at him. So that was it! He had sensed that they had more in common: this must be what he had felt, a kinship that went beyond words. 'Then we are brothers,' he said. 'I am glad.'

'Brothers.' Djeri nodded faintly and closed his eyes; it seemed that talking had tired him. But now, the silence in the room was comfortable. After that awful moment when Djeri had demanded to see his limp, Hopi felt that they understood each other once more.

He must be leaving; the family would soon be returning to visit the invalid. But he had not forgotten his promise to Isis. He placed a hand on Djeri's arm, and the soldier opened his eyes again.

'I must go,' he said. 'But before I do, I have something to ask you about the army camp. Djeri, what is the pit?'

The soldier's response took Hopi by surprise. His body went rigid and he gasped for breath. 'Wha-what do you know about the pit?'

Hopi watched him in alarm. 'Nothing! That's why I'm asking.'

Djeri's hands clutched the covers on the bed. His whole body began to tremble. 'They have sent you . . .' he gulped. 'It's a plot! The gods will have their revenge!'

Hopi was now thoroughly frightened. He stood and grasped Djeri by the shoulder. 'Djeri. Djeri! Stop it!' he begged.

Anty appeared in the doorway. 'What is happening?' he cried. 'Is he worse?'

'I don't know,' said Hopi. 'I don't think he is dying. I think he is losing his mind.'

CHAPTER FIVE

Hopi's chest was heaving by the time he reached Menna's house. The old priest let him in and saw at once that something was wrong.

'Hopi. I was expecting you. Is it Djeri?'

Hopi nodded. 'Yes. He is raving, Menna, and yet he is also sane . . .' He spilled out everything that had happened. 'So the pit has something to do with it all,' he finished. 'But I still have no idea what that could be.'

Menna had listened intently. 'You have done well to come straight to me,' he said. 'For we are servants of the goddess Serqet. I fear that if any of the gods has been angered, it is she.'

'Serqet?' Hopi was puzzled.

'Follow me.'

Menna led Hopi into his sanctuary, where a statue of the goddess sat, along with Menna's cures and

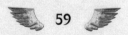

potions. It was peaceful there, but Hopi found that he was unwilling to look too hard at the statue. Any god being angry was bad enough, but their own patron? The thought was terrifying.

The old man went over to a section of the wall where three niches had been cut out of the mud brick. In between the niches hung the shed skins of different types of snake; inside the niches there were more, coiled up, but something else also. Menna reached in and carefully lifted out the dried carcasses of two scorpions.

Scorpions . . . the creatures of the goddess herself. Hopi stared down at them.

'You recognise these?' asked Menna.

'Of course. They're the fat-tailed one and the deathstalker.'

'That's right. And you know what they are capable of doing?'

Hopi nodded. These were two of the most dangerous scorpions in Egypt. Their sting could kill a child, or someone weak; it could bring even a strong man close to death, but not before inflicting the most terrible pain.

'But what do these have to do with Djeri, Menna?'

Menna placed the two dead scorpions back into their niche. 'I cannot be sure,' he said. 'All I can do is piece together the clues. The clearest is the term *pit*. You will have seen the sport of putting scorpions together to fight each other?'

'They make a pit!' Hopi exclaimed.

'Yes.' Menna nodded.

Hopi's mind raced as he considered the implications. If the prisoners of war were sent to a pit, what did that have to do with scorpions? Only one possibility occurred to him, and it was a dreadful one. He didn't want to believe it.

'They are only . . . only Libyans,' he said, but the words sounded hollow.

'No, Hopi.' Menna's voice was sharp. 'Many prisoners of war end up as loyal servants of Egypt. Serqet's creatures should never be abused like this. It is not the way of the goddess Ma'at, either.'

Hopi took a deep breath. So Isis had been right to question the treatment of the prisoners . . . he felt ashamed, now, of dismissing her. 'But what can be done?' he asked.

Menna pursed his lips. 'That remains to be seen. We must first find out if we are right,' he said. 'And to do that, you must go to the army camp with the troupe tonight.'

Isis stood by the storeroom door, listening. She could hear Ramose and Kha playing together out in the courtyard. There was the sound of Kia rhythmically grinding grain. Nefert was singing softly to herself, somewhere upstairs. Isis took one last look around and slipped inside the store. She laid out a little square of old linen cloth on the floor, reached into the basket of fruit and picked out a big handful of dried figs. She dropped them on to the square of linen, then reached for two handfuls of dates and added them to the pile. Hurriedly, she pulled the corners of the cloth together to make a bundle and tied it with a knot at the top. Her heart pounding, she tiptoed to the storeroom door and peered out.

As luck would have it, her brother was just entering the house. Isis ducked back into the store-room – too late. Hopi had already seen her.

'What are you doing in there?' he demanded.

Isis hid the linen bundle behind her back. 'Nothing.'

Hopi laughed. 'You have guilt written all over your face. Show me!' He reached to grab her.

'Don't!' Isis sidestepped, but Hopi managed to see what she was carrying.

'*What?*' He peered at the bundle of fruit. 'What do you need that for?'

'Shhhhhh,' Isis begged him. 'It's not for me.'

Hopi's eyes widened as he realised what she was doing. 'Isis, that's stealing.'

'No! No, it isn't – we're allowed to eat fruit whenever we want.'

'*We* are allowed to eat fruit, yes. But I don't think Nefert and Paneb would be very happy if they knew that you were giving it away. Especially if they knew who you were going to give it to. It's that Libyan girl, isn't it?'

Isis sighed in frustration. She might have known that Hopi would work it out. 'Look,' she whispered, 'I won't eat my share of the fruit for a week. I promise. It's not stealing if I give my own share away, is it?'

Hopi frowned, but he didn't seem *too* angry with her. 'Isis, this prisoner of war thing . . . you might be right. Sort of. Menna wants me to come with you this evening.'

Isis felt a bound of hope. 'Really? Why? Do you know what the pit is?'

Her brother hesitated. 'No. Not yet. That's what I have to find out.'

'But you have some idea?' Isis studied his face.

'Well, yes.'

'Tell me!' Isis demanded.

But Hopi was firm. 'I can't, Isis. Not yet. But if you keep quiet for now and stop pestering, I'll carry your bundle of fruit for you in my linen bag.'

'That's not fair.'

'How else are you going to carry it without anyone noticing?'

Isis hadn't thought of that. She'd only got as far as wanting to help the Libyan girl. But Hopi was right – this was her only option, because he always carried a bag and she never did. Slowly, she nodded. 'But you will tell me later, won't you?'

'I promise I won't keep you in the dark unless I have to.'

Isis gave in. 'All right.' She handed over the bundle and Hopi slipped it into his bag.

The sight of the army camp made Hopi feel small and afraid. Most of the soldiers seemed to be sitting around fires close to their tents, sharpening their weapons or cleaning the horses' harnesses, and he was very conscious of his limp as he passed. The troupe made their way to the central arena, but tonight there were no wrestling matches – just music and dancing while the officers ate their food by the fire. Commander Meref appeared from his tent and ordered the entertainment to begin.

As the troupe took up their instruments, Hopi made a show of holding the women's shawls for a while, as though he were there for a purpose. Then, when he was sure that the officers were absorbed by the performance, he gradually moved backwards until he was shrouded in darkness. He placed the shawls carefully in a pile, then nestled the bundle of fruit on top so that Isis could find it later, and headed away from the arena.

The task he had to face was harder than he had anticipated. When Isis had told him about the wrestling, he had imagined all the soldiers gathered together in one place, but tonight they were spread throughout the camp. It would be difficult to avoid being noticed.

He moved silently towards the darkest part of the camp, ducking behind tents and listening to the soldiers' conversations. Some of them bragged to each other about their greatest feats in battle. Some discussed their favourite wrestlers from the night before. Some were not Egyptian and talked to each other in their own languages.

One particular conversation caught his attention. Staying in the shadow of a tent, he crouched down and peered round it to see two soldiers bent over a fire, talking in low voices.

'. . . That Djeri is dead, or dying, so they say.'

Hopi stiffened and inched closer.

'Perhaps that's why Meref didn't use the pit today.'

'I doubt it. It's his favourite pastime. He didn't

get round to it, that's all.'

The other man pushed a branch further into the fire. 'Maybe you're right.'

The two fell silent for a moment, watching the flames. Hopi's heart was pounding. So there was some connection between Djeri and the pit . . . but what was it? Then one of the soldiers spoke again.

'I keep wondering when he'll use it on us.'

'What? The pit? Never!' The other soldier shook his head. 'He only does it because they're Libyans.'

'I wouldn't be so sure.'

The second soldier shuddered. 'Would Meref really do that to his own men? Anyway, if it's true that Djeri is dead, he'll soon run out of scorpions.'

Hopi almost gasped, but managed to stay quiet.

'There's always someone else who'll catch the beggars.'

'Sure, boys catch 'em when they see 'em. But Djeri was special. Had a knack for finding them. Weird, if you ask me.'

So that was it. Djeri had been Commander Meref's scorpion catcher. Hopi studied the soldiers' faces. They both looked uneasy and fearful.

'We don't *know* Djeri's dead.'

'With his leg cut up like that? Sure he's dead.' The soldier jerked his head back, indicating the linen enclosure behind them. 'That Libyan, though. D'you think he'll survive?'

His companion shook his head. 'Too weak already. The pit will finish him.'

Hopi stared at the enclosure. So the pit was right here and these men were its guards. Silently, he shrank back. He got up and crept around to the other side. He could see now that it was open to the stars, the rough linen pegged out around a series of stakes. Hopi scanned the area for more guards, but all he could see was the glow from the fire on the other side, where the two soldiers still sat. He stepped closer. The fabric of the enclosure came only as high as his chest; he could see over the top.

The troupe's music drifted over the encampment, bright and full of joy, but what he saw in the moonlight made Hopi's heart go cold. In the middle of the enclosure, a young man stood in a knee-high pit. He was tied to a stake. His head was lolling to one side, his mouth hanging open in exhaustion. Hopi took in the dark beard and the brightly coloured robe that had been ripped and torn.

He's just a Libyan prisoner, he told himself. But now that he could see the man in the flesh, he understood how Isis had felt. He saw how the ropes were cutting into his wrists and how his whole body was twisted against the stake. His heart filled with pity.

He looked around the rest of the enclosure. It was almost empty, apart from the man and the stake. But then Hopi saw a box lying in the sand near the edge of the pit. He stared at it. Could it be what he was looking for?

The faint sound of clapping reached his ears. The troupe had just finished one of their routines. Hopi took a deep breath and dropped to his knees. The linen was pulled tight between the stakes, but with a little easing and some scraping in the sandy earth, Hopi got an arm beneath it. He rolled on to his back, and ducked his head under.

He stopped. The prisoner had heard him. He was staring at Hopi, wild-eyed. With his free arm, Hopi lifted a finger to his lips, begging the man to stay quiet. The prisoner obeyed, his expression changing from fear to curiosity as Hopi slowly pulled his whole body into the enclosure. He was in. He dragged his bag through after him and lay still for a moment, listening to the murmur of the guards' voices. Their fire crackled, their conversation continued. Nothing had alerted them yet.

Hopi lifted himself up off his belly, but stayed doubled over and hobbled as quickly as he could towards the box. He reached it and dropped to his knees once more.

A harsh, unintelligible sound came out of the Libyan's throat. Hopi glared at him, shaking his head furiously and tapping his lips with his finger.

'What was that?' said one of the soldiers, the sound of his voice just reaching Hopi's ears.

There was nowhere to hide. Hopi could feel himself sweating. He waited for the soldiers to get up and check the enclosure. The Libyan's face was still rigid with fear. Seconds passed. Nothing happened. Hopi heard the murmur of the men resuming their conversation and let out a long sigh of relief. It was time to investigate the box.

Hopi reached out and touched its lid, running his hand along the edge. Although the box was rough, the lid was well made and close-fitting. Hopi got his fingernails underneath it and slowly lifted it. A shaft of moonlight lit up the interior. It was just as Menna had thought. Inside, scuttling around the bottom, were three deathstalker scorpions.

Hopi knew what he should do. He should close the lid and report back to Menna. But how could he do that, with the Libyan staring at him in terror? He had to do something – and do it fast. Handling scorpions like these was very risky. Their sting, as Commander Meref clearly knew only too well, would cause intense pain and convulsions at the very least. Hopi made his decision. He whipped his basket out of his bag and settled it firmly into the sand. He removed the lid, then lifted the wooden box and tipped the scorpions out, shaking it hard to make sure that they fell. When he was sure that all three were in his basket, he rammed the lid over them.

He replaced the empty box exactly where he'd found it. And then, with a small, sympathetic nod towards the Libyan, he made for the fence and scrabbled back under it, disappearing into the night the way he had come.

No wrestling. Isis hadn't reckoned on that. It was a disaster. How was she going to visit the Libyan girl now? As she danced alongside Mut, her mind was working furiously. She had to get away. She just *had* to. She watched the officers out of the corner of her eye, looking for any signs that they would ask for the entertainment to end.

Commander Meref seemed bored. He sat facing the troupe, but his eyes weren't focused on the dancing. They had a distant look, as though he were thinking about something else. And as Isis sneaked more glances at the men, she noticed that none of the officers seemed to be very interested in the troupe, either. It was odd – they were all watching the commander, then turning to each other to exchange opinions, then glancing back at him again. It was as though they were waiting for something.

Abruptly, the commander stood up. He raised a hand. Nefert, Sheri and Kia stopped playing, while Isis and Mut came to a halt.

'Enough for now,' he said, and passed a hand over his forehead, as though the music had wearied him.

Isis eyed the pile of shawls that Hopi had left by the side of the arena. She knew that her bundle of fruit would be tucked in among them. She watched as the officers waited expectantly for the commander to speak.

'Fetch the prisoner,' he ordered. 'The music is giving me a headache. I would rather watch some real entertainment.'

A murmur rippled among the officers. One of them clicked his fingers to a pair of guards, who came running. Then the officer turned to Commander Meref. 'Should we go to the pit, sir?'

The commander shook his head impatiently. 'No, no. Bring everything here. Set some soldiers to work. They can dig, can't they?'

'But this is the wrestling arena. To dig a pit would ruin it,' said the officer nervously.

'If they can dig a hole, they can fill it in again. Get on with it!' barked Commander Meref.

The officer flinched and immediately sent for more soldiers. The guards disappeared towards another part of the camp. Isis wondered where Hopi could be. He had gone to find out about the pit, but whatever it was, it was about to happen right here! Her eyes roved the shadows, looking for her brother, but there was no sign of him.

Soldiers appeared with tools and began to dig the earth in the centre of the arena. The commander had given the troupe no further orders and the three women were discussing what to do with Paneb. They looked as though they were waiting for a chance to speak to Meref. Perhaps they would be sent home early again! While Mut watched the soldiers digging, Isis slipped away from the troupe and grabbed her bundle from the pile of shawls. Now was her only chance – and she had to be quick.

She ran lightly across the camp, taking less care than she had the night before. All she could think of was that she had to help the Libyan girl before Nefert and Paneb started looking for her – and before the girl's brother was brought to the pit. Now she was running headlong, ignoring the shadows in her haste.

It was a big mistake. From behind a chariot, a

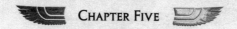

soldier stepped out, barring her path. Isis knew she was fast – she had dodged people before. She ducked down and made to run past him. But this was no ordinary soldier. He grabbed her arm and spun her round so that she was brought up close to him. Gasping with fear, she stared up into his face.

'Where do you think you're going?' he demanded.

It was Nes the Lion, the great wrestler they had watched the night before.

CHAPTER SIX

Hopi made his way to the edge of the camp. Reappearing at the side of the arena was too risky – he wanted to get the deathstalkers right away, in case someone started asking questions. As he checked the periphery for guards, his heart sank. They were stationed at regular intervals along the boundary. What was worse, the surroundings were flat and featureless, with few rocks and fewer trees. Even if he managed to get out, the guards would see him as he made for Waset. He thought of Isis and her tale of the Libyan's attempted escape: no wonder he had been caught so easily.

Two chariots stood idle nearby. Hopi crawled between them to watch and wait. At least no one would notice that the scorpions had gone. The officers were watching the performers . . . and then he went still. The music had stopped. There was nothing but the sound of voices in the distance, and the steady rhythm of a horse chewing its fodder somewhere close by.

Hopi listened, straining his ears. Why had the entertainment finished early? *Had* it finished early? He heard shouts. Something was happening at the arena.

The guards were on full alert. News was beginning to buzz among the soldiers sitting by their tents, and the message soon reached the lookouts.

'They're digging a pit in the arena!' came the cry.

A pit. Hopi's heart thudded. If they were digging a pit, perhaps they were going to use the deathstalkers tonight. He had to get away. It would only be minutes before they realised what they had lost.

The guards near Hopi had left their positions. All their attention was fixed on the centre of the camp. They gathered together, gossiping and forgetting their strict formation. Hopi spotted his opportunity. Keeping as low as he could, he ran for the gap behind the neglectful guards, then half-ran, half-limped for the only cover he could see – an acacia tree near the road back to Waset.

Isis tried to wriggle out of the wrestler's grasp, but he was much too strong for her.

'You're coming with me,' he said in a low voice. He

75

picked her up and tucked her under his arm as though she were just a toy.

Isis wondered whether to scream, but the thought of Commander Meref stopped her. She clutched the bundle of fruit and tried to think of a good excuse, but fear muddled her thoughts.

Nes carried her through the flap of a small, dark tent and dumped her on to a mat.

'Please, let me go back to the troupe,' begged Isis. 'They don't know where I am.'

The wrestler reached outside for a flaming torch that was stuck into the ground, and the tent filled with flickering light. Isis took in the dagger that lay near her feet and a shield propped against the wall of the tent, splattered with something dark and sticky. She guessed it was blood.

'That doesn't surprise me,' said Nes. 'I can spot a girl who's up to mischief.'

'I wasn't!' protested Isis.

'Really?' Nes gave a slow smile. 'We'll soon see about that. Show me what you were carrying.'

Isis looked up at him. His muscles were enormous and his bulk seemed to fill the whole tent. All the same, behind the deep lines and the stern set of his mouth, there was a hint of something softer.

She bowed her head. 'It's only fruit,' she whispered. She bent to undo the bundle. 'Look. It's just figs and dates. They can't do anyone any harm.'

Nes crouched down beside her. His big fingers reached for one of the figs and popped it into his mouth. 'Mmm,' he said. 'Tastiest fig I've had in a long time. Did you bring them especially for me?' He reached for another one.

'No, I didn't! Don't – they're not for you –' Isis stopped.

'Do you know who I am?' Nes asked.

Isis nodded. 'Yes. You're Nes, the Lion. You're a great wrestler. We saw you last night.'

Nes held the second fig up to the light and rolled it around with his rough, calloused fingers. 'So who in this camp deserves figs and dates more than me? He must be very important.'

'It's not a he.'

Now Nes looked genuinely surprised. 'But we are all men.'

'They are for one of the Libyan girls,' confessed Isis. 'One of the prisoners of war.'

Nes frowned. 'You have taken this risk for a prisoner?'

Bravely, Isis raised her eyes to his. 'I wanted to help her, that's all. Is that really so wicked?'

The wrestler regarded Isis with a troubled

expression. 'Well, no, it's not *wicked*.'

Isis felt a bound of hope. Perhaps it would all work out. Perhaps Nes would let her get away with her escapade. 'There, I've told you,' she said. 'And you can keep some of the figs. But, please, will you let me go now? They're digging a pit in the arena and –'

'They are doing *what*?' Nes pounced on her words and Isis cowered back.

'They've just started,' she squeaked. 'Commander Meref stopped the dancing . . .' She trailed off.

The enormous wrestler was listening to the sounds of the camp. He reminded Isis of a wild animal, his senses tuned to the slightest movement. Voices and the faint clank of bronze tools drifted across from the arena. Nes sat perfectly still for a moment. Then his great body sprang into action.

'Come. I shall take you back there,' he said, grabbing Isis by the hand. 'And we shall see about this pit-digging!'

Hopi had a stitch in his side by the time he reached the outskirts of Waset, and his lungs were bursting. But he had done it: he had managed to get away without any of the soldiers chasing him. He slowed to a walk and painfully made his way to Menna's house. It was late now, but he knew that his tutor would want to hear the news.

Menna came to the door holding an oil lamp. 'Come in, come in. I was hoping you would report back quickly,' he said, and led the way into his sanctuary. He placed the lamp in one of the wall niches and indicated the mats. 'Sit down. What have you discovered?'

Hopi flopped on to the mats, wincing as he manoeuvred his bad leg underneath him. He reached for his bag and opened it. 'You were right, Menna. I found deathstalkers – three.'

Menna's forehead creased into a frown as his apprentice brought out his basket. 'You took them?'

'Yes.' Hopi looked up at his tutor nervously. 'I know I probably shouldn't have, but the prisoner was there, all tied up. I couldn't just leave him to be tortured, could I?'

Menna shook his head approvingly. 'No. You were absolutely right. But it raises the stakes. We now have the wrath of the army to deal with.'

'They don't know it was me,' said Hopi. 'I managed to get out of the camp without anyone noticing.'

The old man stroked his chin. 'Hmm. Yes, perhaps. But it will not take a genius to work it out.' He waved a hand at the basket. 'Come, then. Show me.'

Carefully, Hopi took off the lid of the basket.

Menna reached for the oil lamp, and together they peered inside. The three scorpions were piled on top of each other at the bottom of the basket and began scrabbling around as the light fell on them.

'Such amazing creatures,' murmured Menna. 'You see how their pincers are quite small, smaller than those of other scorpions? This is because the death-stalker's sting is the most powerful of all. It does not need large pincers to subdue its prey.'

Hopi watched one of the scorpions curl its tail over its head – the tail with the deadly sting at its tip. 'Is there a cure for such a sting?' he asked.

'There are some herbs,' said Menna. 'But for a severe sting, the only cure is magic. There is a series of spells. Once they have been spoken, the fate of the victim lies with Serqet herself.'

'You haven't taught me these spells, Menna.'

The old priest looked thoughtful. 'No, I haven't. They are the most powerful of all the spells of Serqet.'

Hopi had now spent many, many hours mashing herbs, onions and minerals together to make cures for snake bites. He had been out collecting everything from carob to terebinth to add to them. But of all the cures he had mastered in his time with Menna, Hopi loved learning spells best. He badly wanted to learn these powerful ones.

'Am I ready?' he asked quietly.

One of the deathstalkers was trying to creep up the sides of the basket and make its escape. Its yellowish pincers groped the air. With a small wooden stick, Menna pushed it back to join its fellows in the depths of the container.

'Yes, Hopi,' he said. 'I think you are.'

'Thank you,' breathed Hopi. 'Can we start now?'

It was late. Menna looked tired and Hopi expected him to defer the training until the morning. But to his surprise, the old priest nodded. 'Yes. Then you can meditate upon the incantations through the night. Something tells me that you may need this knowledge before long. Let us begin at once.'

And to Hopi's fascination and delight, he reached for a scroll of well-worn papyrus.

Back at the arena, pandemonium had broken out. Guards had brought the prisoner of war before Commander Meref, but the Libyan was not all they had brought. They had come with shocking news, too. It spread among the soldiers like wildfire and they milled around, talking in excited voices.

'The scorpions have gone!' Isis heard one of them shout.

'The gods have spoken!' cried another.

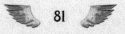

Isis looked up at Nes. 'What scorpions are they talking about?' she asked, thinking at once of Hopi. If scorpions had disappeared, he would be the first person she'd suspect.

The great wrestler looked down at her and shook his head grimly. 'This is army business. It is not something that a girl should know about.'

'Does it have anything to do with the pit?' Isis insisted.

'Never you mind about that,' Nes told her.

'But I need to know.' Isis was desperate to get to the bottom of it. 'What's going to happen to the prisoner who was caught last night?'

Now Nes looked down at her in astonishment. 'How do you know about him?'

'We were here when he tried to escape,' Isis reminded him. 'He's the brother of the girl I wanted to help.'

Nes stared at her for a second, then shook his head. 'You know far too much,' he said. He began elbowing his way through the excited soldiers to the edge of the arena, where Nefert, Sheri and Kia were scanning the crowd with worried expressions. Isis knew at once that they were looking for her. She turned quickly to the wrestler.

'Please, take these,' she said, offering him the

bundle of fruit. 'You know who they were meant for. I can't take them back home again. Please deliver them for me, if you can.'

She could see that Nes's mind was already elsewhere. His gaze had rested on the soldiers who were steadily digging up a section of the arena, and his eyes blazed with anger. Isis persisted, pressing the bundle into his hands.

For an instant, he glanced down at the fruit, then looked into her eyes. 'Leave them with me,' he said. 'And if you are feeling brave, meet me again, little dancer. Tomorrow at noon.'

Nefert had spotted Isis now and was beckoning furiously.

'Tomorrow, but . . . where?' Isis asked, waving back at Nefert.

'On the town side of Ipet-Resyt temple,' said the wrestler. 'I'll be there.' Then he left her, marching over to confront the digging soldiers.

Isis ran to Nefert and Sheri.

'Isis! There you are. We must leave at once.' Nefert looked shaken. 'I have had enough of this place. These men – they do not treat us with respect.'

The women had already put on their shawls, while Paneb was trying to get Commander Meref's attention. It was a hopeless task. The commander was listening to ten soldiers all trying to speak to him at once.

'Where *were* you?' whispered Mut, clutching Isis's arm. 'And where did Hopi go?'

'I don't know,' Isis whispered back. She felt a pang of fear for her brother. Then she reflected: surely if he had been caught, he would have been dragged here by now? She had seen enough of the camp to know that anything unusual was reported to the commander. 'I think he must have already left.'

'They're all talking about scorpions,' said Mut. 'I bet he has something to do with that, don't you? Well, don't you? Tell me, Isis.'

'I don't *know*,' said Isis. 'Honestly, I don't.'

They watched as Paneb made one last attempt to speak to the commander. It was no good. Commander Meref swatted him off as though he were an irritating fly. Paneb turned away and rejoined the troupe.

'Let's go,' he said, his voice full of disgust. 'This was a bad idea from the outset. Last night we were sent home early. Tonight they are preparing some horrible entertainment that seems to have gone wrong.'

'I agree,' said Nefert. 'This is no place for Isis and Mut. These men are savages. I gather they take pleasure in baiting scorpions.' She shuddered.

Sheri and Kia said nothing. But Isis noticed that

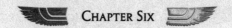

they stayed close together as they all left the camp.
And, as they passed the final fire before stepping into
the darkness that lay between them and Waset, she
saw the silver streak of a tear on Sheri's cheek.

CHAPTER SEVEN

Hopi woke with a start. His neck was stiff. He sat up, rubbing it, and saw that he had fallen asleep on the mats in Menna's sanctuary, with an oil lamp still burning and the papyrus sheets of spells spread out around him. He yawned and stretched. All was quiet. It must be the middle of the night. Then he peered outside and saw that the first grey light of dawn was filtering into the courtyard.

He gathered the papyrus sheets and scrolled them up again. Menna had taken him through the spells carefully, step by step, explaining each hieroglyph as they went. Hopi still had a long way to go to catch up on his schooling, and many of the signs were unfamiliar to him. But as they had chanted the incantations, repeating them over and over, he had felt the knowledge seeping in.

The light in the courtyard was growing brighter. Hopi put the scrolls back into the niche where they belonged, whispering the spells again to check that he had remembered them. They came back easily, their rhythms swinging through his mind. It was a good feeling. He felt a little awed, too, that he was now the guardian of such magic.

The soft rumble of Menna's snores drifted from a room at the back of the house. Hopi looked around the sanctuary for his bag, but the priest must have moved it. No matter; the scorpions were safe here. He would come back later. For now, he must return home. He slipped out of the house as the first rays of sun warmed the deserted streets. A donkey brayed; the town would soon come to life.

Hopi walked slowly, thinking through all that had happened since the previous morning. He thought about the pit. What a ghastly sport – goading death-stalkers into stinging prisoners of war. It would be kinder to kill them outright.

And then he thought about Djeri. He knew a lot more about the soldier now. He was clearly a skilled scorpion handler and Commander Meref had made use of that skill. But it was still confusing. He had felt so much sympathy for the soldier at first, but Djeri's reaction to his limp had been very hurtful. And now this. How could Hopi have warmed to a man who had been part of something so terrible?

He reached home and found the household just beginning to stir. Isis and Mut had slept on the roof and were still huddled in their linen covers, waking up slowly in the morning sun.

'Where did *you* go?' demanded Mut at once. 'Was it you who took the scorpions?'

Hopi was startled. He hadn't realised that his actions would be so obvious. 'What scorpions?' he bluffed, throwing a quick glance at Isis. He knew she wouldn't be fooled.

'Don't try to be clever,' said Mut. 'Why else did Menna send you to the camp?'

Hopi sat down next to them on the mats. He couldn't deny it, but he knew he had to be careful what he said in front of Mut. 'It was *information* that Menna wanted,' he said. 'I left quite early to talk to him. Did you hear any of the soldiers talking about me?'

Isis shook her head. 'No. We just had to leave.'

'So you didn't finish performing?'

'No,' said Mut. 'Father's very fed up with them. Well, we all are. We're not going back to the camp again.'

Hopi sneaked another look at Isis, wondering how she'd got on with her Libyan prisoner girl. He guessed she would be very disappointed not to be visiting the camp for a third time but, if anything, she seemed quite cheerful. In fact, Hopi spotted a secret gleam in her eye, and suddenly he guessed the truth. He knew his sister all too well. She was up to something.

Isis was on tenterhooks all morning. She was desperate to find out what had really happened to Hopi and to tell him about meeting Nes, but she didn't get the chance. Her brother was tired. He ate some flatbread for breakfast and promptly fell asleep. Isis squinted up at the sun every few minutes. She would need to make up an excuse to leave the house just before noon. Meanwhile, she got on with sweeping the courtyard and steps, trying not to think about the meeting that would soon take place.

But it didn't escape her notice that all three women were looking very glum. Sheri and Kia usually bustled about doing chores, but today they sat in the courtyard doing nothing in particular.

The sweeping finished, she joined Mut on the first floor, where her dance partner was sorting out the troupe's large collection of oil and perfume bottles. Isis tried to help, but found that her fingers were shaking. She was sure that if she carried on she would end up breaking something.

'This bottle's nearly empty,' she announced to Mut, holding up a bottle of almond oil. Then she had a brainwave. 'I'll ask Nefert if I can go and buy some more in the market.'

'Go on, then,' Mut responded. 'You're only making a mess of the sorting.'

Isis got to her feet, gripping the bottle tightly. She ran down the steps. The courtyard was empty – not even the boys were there. She looked into the back room, then moved on to the front. There was no sign of either Nefert, her two sons, or Kia. There was only Sheri, taking things out of a wooden casket.

'Oh!' exclaimed Isis. 'Where is everyone?'

Sheri didn't turn to look at her. 'Nefert and Kia have gone visiting with the boys,' she said, with her back to Isis.

Her voice sounded strange, sort of muffled. Isis studied her. Suddenly, from the tension in her shoulders, she realised that Sheri was crying again.

She stepped closer. 'Are you all right, Sheri?' she asked.

The older woman gave a loud sniff. 'I'm sorry, Isis. I'm fine, really.'

'Oh, Sheri.' Isis put the oil bottle on the floor and rushed to give her a hug.

Sheri hugged her back and Isis heard a sob. Sheri

cried for a few moments, then controlled herself. 'It's so silly, after all this time . . .'

'No, it isn't!' declared Isis. 'I still cry for Mother and Father. So does Hopi. I know he does.' She looked up into Sheri's gentle face. 'I wish I could help you, though. I wish we were going back to the camp. We might have found something out.'

Sheri shook her head briskly. 'No, no, Isis. It's quite all right. It just brought back memories, that's all. But I shall put everything away again now.'

It was then that Isis noticed what she was holding. The casket was full of Sheri's belongings and, dangling from her fingers, was a weapon made of bronze. It was an ornamental dagger.

'Was that your husband's?' Isis asked in awe.

Sheri nodded and sighed. She held it out, flat, for Isis to see. 'Yes. It belonged to Henu.'

'Henu? That was his name?' Isis stroked the blade in wonder. The handle was carved into the shape of a lotus flower at the end, with several *ankhs*, the symbol of eternal life, entwined with patterns further down. It was beautiful. She tested the edge of the blade.

'Careful!' exclaimed Sheri, and Isis jumped back. It was still razor sharp.

A drop of bright red blood welled up. 'It's only a scratch,' said Isis, looking down at the blood, then sucking her finger.

'I'd better put it away.' Sheri reached for the leather scabbard.

Isis watched as Sheri wrapped the dagger in linen and put it back into her box. She frowned. The blood had made her think of something. The dagger seemed oddly familiar, but how could it? It didn't seem possible. She was sure that Sheri had never shown it to her before.

Hopi leaned over the low wall that ran around the roof of the house, watching the street below, with the new spells still running through his head. As he muttered the last one to himself, he saw Isis leave the house and hurry up the street.

'Isis!' he called after her.

His sister stopped and looked up.

'Where are you going?' he demanded.

She waved an ointment bottle at him. 'I'm going to buy almond oil.'

'And what else are you doing?'

Isis grinned. She looked up and down the street to see who was listening, then stepped closer to the wall before answering, 'Walk with me to the market and I'll tell you.'

'Fine.' Hopi looked around for his bag, which he

always carried. Then he remembered – he'd left it at Menna's. He popped his head over the wall again. 'Coming.'

He hopped down the stairs and joined his sister on the street. As soon as they were out of earshot of the house Isis told him how Nes the wrestler had caught her in the camp, and that she was on her way to see him again.

'You're going to meet one of the *wrestlers*? Isis!' Hopi was full of concern.

'It's fine, Hopi, honestly,' said Isis. 'I'm meeting him right outside the temple, where the whole town can see. That can't be dangerous, can it?'

'Well . . .' Hopi thought about it. The truth was that Isis was very good at extricating herself from difficult situations – better than he was sometimes. 'Just don't go following him to anywhere you can't get away from easily.'

'I won't,' Isis reassured him. 'Anyway, what happened to you last night? *Did* you have anything to do with the scorpions they were talking about?'

Hopi recounted his story about the deathstalkers and how he had taken them from the camp. His sister's eyes grew round with horror as the truth about the pit sank in.

'But that's *awful!*' she gasped. 'Is that really what

they were digging a pit for?'

'Seems like it, yes.' Hopi knew that Isis would be aghast. 'But they couldn't do it without the scorpions. That's something, isn't it?'

'I'm so glad!' said Isis fervently. 'But what will happen now? Won't Commander Meref punish the Libyan some other way?'

Hopi hadn't really thought about that. He frowned. 'Maybe. But nothing can be as bad as a deathstalker's sting.'

His sister's face was sad. 'How terrible to be a prisoner,' she said.

Now, Hopi had to agree. And he felt ashamed that he had ever felt otherwise.

They had reached a junction, and Hopi stopped.

'I'll leave you here,' he said. 'I'm going to see Menna. Good luck with Nes. And be careful, Isis.'

'I will,' Isis promised him again.

Hopi limped off down the side street. He *did* want to see Menna, but part of him knew that he was avoiding someone else – and that was Djeri. He was dreading having to confront the soldier with what he knew. But maybe, if he talked it through with his tutor, Menna would give him some strength and guidance. He hoped so, anyway.

He reached the old priest's house. He usually

knocked, then let himself in; it was the pattern they had established, for Menna often had his hands full. But now he pushed the door and nothing happened. It stayed firmly shut. Hopi was puzzled. Menna had said nothing about going out visiting. He knocked again, hammering harder this time. All was silent. Hopi banged and shoved on the door, but there was no doubt about it. It was firmly barred, and Menna wasn't in.

Isis made quick work of buying the oil in the market. After driving a hard bargain, she asked the vendor if she could leave her purchase with him and pick it up later. Then she hurried off towards the temple of Ipet-Resyt.

The sun was almost directly overhead now. She was worried that she might miss Nes altogether, and broke into a jog as she approached the great temple, its vast walls and gates brilliant white in the sun. Nes had said to meet him on the town side, which meant the back of the temple, but the building was enormous. She started at the south end and made her way up, her heart thudding with nerves. Now that she was here, she couldn't imagine why he had arranged to meet her.

He was already there waiting. Isis spotted him

halfway along the temple wall. Somehow, set against the normal people of the town who bustled past him, he seemed even bigger and more muscle-bound than he had in the camp. Isis swallowed. Was it really wise to trust him?

It was too late for thoughts like that. Nes had seen her. He raised his hand and waved. Pushing her fear aside, Isis went towards him.

He chuckled as she drew close. 'You're brave for a little dancer,' he said. 'I reckoned I'd seen the last of you.'

Isis watched him warily. 'I hope you didn't eat all the fruit,' she said.

From behind his back, Nes produced the bundle that she'd given him the night before. 'Would I do something like that?'

Isis stared at the fruit in dismay. 'But you said you'd give them to her!'

Nes grinned easily. 'Don't fret, little one,' he said. 'I thought you might like to give them to her yourself.' And with that, he began to stride off in the direction of the great avenue.

Isis trotted after him, dumbfounded. How could she give the girl the fruit? Wasn't she still imprisoned in the army camp? Where was he taking her? Clutching the bundle tightly, she struggled to keep up with his massive strides.

Nes reached the front of the temple where the great avenue began, stretching out towards the even greater temple complex of Ipet-Isut. He checked that Isis was still with him, then turned to the right and led her to a walled enclosure. It was made of mud brick and wasn't part of the temple itself, but it was similarly painted, and Isis got the sense that it had something to do with temple worship. They reached an imposing door, and Nes knocked. A beautiful girl answered. She seemed to be expecting them.

'Is this the one you spoke of?' she asked Nes.

'That's right,' the wrestler replied. He turned to Isis. 'Go on in.' Nes gestured towards the door, but stayed where he was.

Isis was perplexed and rather scared. 'But aren't *you* coming?' she asked.

Nes smiled and shook his head. 'Only women are allowed,' he said. 'They'll look after you in there. Don't be afraid.'

Isis looked at the girl, who smiled back at her. 'He's right. You can trust us. Come.'

There didn't seem to be much option. Isis took a deep breath and stepped over the threshold. The girl led her across a deserted courtyard, then along a dim corridor. Somewhere up ahead, Isis heard the sound of sweet singing.

'What *is* this place?' she whispered to the girl.

The girl turned, her smile soft and tranquil. 'We are priestesses of Hathor,' she replied.

'Hathor?' As far as Isis was concerned, the great temples of Waset were dedicated to Amun-Re, Mut and Khonsu.

'There is a small shrine to Hathor deep inside the temple,' explained the girl. 'But this is where we purify foreigners, for of course, they cannot enter the temple itself.'

Isis was still completely lost. 'I don't know what you mean,' she said.

The young priestess was very patient. 'No Egyptian man wants a dirty, bedraggled slave,' she explained. 'Here they are washed and shaved. We oil their skin and dress them in clean linen. You have come to see one of them, haven't you?'

So that was it. They came out into another, smaller courtyard, and Isis gasped. It was a hive of activity. Priestesses padded to and fro carrying bowls of scented water; others carried piles of fresh linen; three sang hymns in a corner. And there, in the centre of the courtyard, sat all the female prisoners of war.

CHAPTER EIGHT

'Come,' said the young priestess. 'I will take you to the girl you seek.'

Isis had been eyeing the group of women, trying to spot the Libyan girl. The priestess led her across the courtyard and, all at once, Isis was standing in front of her. Her mouth dropped open in surprise. The girl was almost unrecognisable. Her long, tangled hair was gone and she wore a neat black Egyptian wig. The torn stripy dress that she had worn had been replaced with a gown of simple white linen. Instead of being covered in dust, her skin was clean and shining with oil, and her eyes had been outlined in black kohl. Isis was astonished. She would easily pass for an Egyptian on the street.

The girl looked at Isis with barely veiled hostility, and said nothing.

'Her name is Neith,' said the priestess of Hathor. 'Do you wish to tell her yours?'

'Isis,' she whispered faintly, still in shock.

The priestess spoke a few words in the girl's language. Neith listened, then responded, her voice sharp and questioning.

'She wants to know what you want with her,' the priestess translated. 'She's asking who you are.'

'But she saw me . . .' Isis began. Then she thought back. The only time that she had actually connected with Neith was on the track out of Waset, when they had locked gazes for a few seconds. Neith had no idea that Isis had spied on her in the enclosure, witnessed her brother's arrest, or returned the next night with fruit.

Tentatively, she held out her gift. 'Tell her that I'm the girl she saw near the camp and that . . . I'm sorry.' Then she felt stuck. What else could she possibly say? Neith's brother was in a dreadful situation, and her own wasn't much better – she was about to become someone's slave, and there was nothing that Isis could do about it.

Neith took the bundle, but now Isis felt ashamed of it. The linen was very grubby. It had been taken out to the camp, left with Nes and carried back again. She watched as the Libyan girl put it down by her side without opening it, then looked at Isis with a question in her eyes. Isis could read her look.

Is that all? Neith seemed to say.

Isis now felt like running away. This was all a big, embarrassing mistake. She turned to the priestess. 'That's all I came for,' she said. 'I can go now.'

The priestess looked puzzled. 'Well, if you're sure. Of course.' And she spoke briefly to Neith again.

Isis started walking back towards the exit, her head bowed.

But then the priestess called, 'Wait.'

The women were all watching her, their unhappy eyes following her every step. Isis felt her cheeks blazing, but she turned round to face the priestess again.

'Neith says thank you,' said the priestess. 'She's glad that you came.'

'That's all right.' Isis tried to smile.

Neith touched the bundle of fruit. She smiled back, but her lower lip was trembling and her kohl-rimmed eyes were brimming with tears.

Hopi wandered the streets of Waset aimlessly, attracting local children who hoped he'd show them a snake. He shrugged and laughed, showing them that he had nothing with him.

But inside, he wasn't laughing. He felt guilty,

angry and confused. With no Menna to consult, he had to think for himself. He knew he must go and see Djeri, if only to change his dressings. He was putting it off and his cowardice made him feel guilty. But the more he thought about the deathstalkers, the more his anger with Djeri swelled. The feelings swirled around inside him and, at last, Hopi knew he could avoid them no longer. He changed direction and made for Anty's house.

Anty seemed pleased to see him. 'Come in, come in,' he said. 'Djeri has been asking for you.'

The news made Hopi feel worse. 'How is he?' he asked.

'He is calmer,' said Anty. 'And there is no fever. In other words, he is much better. We feel the danger has passed. Thank you, Hopi.'

Hopi was tongue-tied for a moment. 'I'm glad.'

Anty smiled and led him to his son's room.

The soldier was awake, but Hopi avoided his gaze as he walked in.

'Hopi. I'm happy to see you,' Djeri greeted him.

Hopi reached for the honey and oil that he had left next to the bed. He didn't know what to say, so instead he reached for the covers and pulled them back. Still saying nothing, he began to inspect Djeri's leg.

'You are not going to greet me?' asked the soldier.

Hopi looked up. He licked his lips. This was even more difficult than he had imagined. 'I have been to the army camp,' he said quietly. 'I know what you have done.'

Djeri stared at him and then a slow, soft sigh escaped from his lips. 'Is that so,' he said. 'Well, it is better that someone knows. Now you can leave me to die and to receive the punishment I deserve in the Next World.'

Hopi looked down at Djeri's leg. It was still a nasty, glistening mess, but in spite of everything, he could see that it was likely to heal – in time.

'I don't think that the gods require your life,' he said. 'I have already told you: you will be a cripple, like me.'

He added a little more oil and honey to the wounds, then covered Djeri's legs again and went to sit by his side.

The silence slowly thickened. It was hot, and flies buzzed around the room. Outside, the soft call of laughing doves rose and fell. Hopi found that he was growing even more upset. At last, he could bear it no longer.

'How could you do such a thing?' he burst out. 'I thought I had found a brother. I thought we could learn from each other. I would have supported you, I would have helped you cope with your wounds.'

'And now you will not?' Djeri's voice was flat.

Hopi felt close to tears. 'Just tell me. Why did you do it?' he whispered.

The soldier shifted on the bed, trying to get more comfortable. 'I have always been a scorpion catcher,' he said. 'Even when I was a small boy, I would catch them for my friends and we would keep them imprisoned. Sometimes, we made them fight each other and wagered on which one would win.'

Hopi listened. 'Many boys do this,' he commented. 'You were not unusual.'

'No,' agreed Djeri. 'The difference is that I carried my interest into adulthood. My brothers were my father's apprentices; they followed in his footsteps to become scribes. I was the third son, with no future, and so the army was the best option. I joined young, and soon found that my fellow soldiers enjoyed my hobby as much as my boyhood friends had done.'

'But there is nothing wrong in that,' said Hopi, still hoping that, somehow, Djeri could prove himself innocent.

'Nothing at all. But I did well in the army. I moved on from the infantry and became a charioteer. My strength and bravery came to the attention of the platoon leader, and soon afterwards, Commander Meref himself began to notice me. He soon heard of my skill with scorpions. It was then that things began to go wrong.'

Djeri's voice was dry, and Hopi reached for some beer. He helped the soldier to drink, then prompted him again. 'Go on.'

'What more can I say?' demanded Djeri. 'The commander must be obeyed.'

They lapsed into silence again. Hopi mulled it over, trying to work out what to think. Couldn't Djeri have refused to catch any more scorpions? Couldn't he have released them when he knew what they were being used for?

'You still had a choice,' he said eventually.

Now Djeri seemed to be getting angry. 'Yes, soldiers have a choice,' he responded bitterly. 'Let me tell you what it is. To obey, or to disobey. To live, or to die. Very simple, isn't it? What do you know about choices such as those?'

Hopi's thoughts were reeling. 'I-I don't know,' he stammered. 'Nothing, I suppose.'

'Well, there you are, then.' Djeri rested his head on his pillow again, and closed his eyes.

The priestess of Hathor led Isis back through the deserted courtyard.

'What will happen to her?' demanded Isis.

The priestess shook her head. 'We do what the army wants of us. What happens after that is not our concern.' They reached the door and the woman opened it.

'But can't you look after the women here?' Isis asked. 'You'd look after them properly, wouldn't you?'

The priestess smiled sadly. 'They do not belong to us,' she said. 'They will go where the army decides to send them.' And with that, she ushered Isis out on to the street.

Nes was waiting for her, crouching down on his haunches and whittling a stick with a little knife. 'All done?' He stood up. 'That was quick.'

Isis looked up into his face. 'I don't understand,' she said. 'Whose slaves are they going to be? Why can't they stay here with the priestesses?'

Nes gave a lopsided smile. 'And what use would they be inside there?' he asked. 'No, little dancer. These women belong to us – the soldiers. They are our reward for the harsh life we lead. They will be distributed among us, according to how well we have fought. Their fate, and that of the men, will be decided tomorrow morning.'

'Oh.' Isis felt helpless and sad. Then a thought occurred to her. Nes was older than most soldiers, and a great warrior. 'So you must have many slaves already.'

'That's right,' said Nes. 'They work on my farm while I'm away fighting.'

'You have a farm?'

Nes spread his hands. 'I am the Lion,' he said, as though that explained everything.

They began to walk back along the length of the great temple. Nes took enormous strides and Isis skipped to keep up with him.

'Please wait,' she gasped breathlessly.

'Of course.' Nes spun round and smiled. 'Sorry, little dancer.'

But now, Isis stopped in her tracks. She stared. As he had turned, the end of the soldier's kilt had flapped to one side, revealing a weapon underneath. It had been there before, of course, jutting up, but Nes's arm had mostly hidden it. Now a memory slotted into place. Isis thought back . . . yes, that was right. She had seen it only the night before – in Nes's tent. And it was exactly the same as the one that Sheri had shown her.

'Nes,' she said slowly, 'did you ever know a soldier called Henu?'

The soldier's face went still. Involuntarily, his hand moved to the dagger and rested on the lotus-shaped hilt. 'Why do you ask?'

'I have seen another dagger just like that one,' said

Isis, pointing. 'It was carved in exactly the same way. And it belonged to a soldier called Henu.'

'When? When did you see this?' Nes dropped to his knees and grasped Isis by the shoulders.

'Today,' said Isis. He was now at her level and she could look directly into his eyes. 'He was the husband of Sheri, one of the musicians I work with.'

Nes's grip slackened and he gazed over her shoulder. 'Impossible. It can't be . . .' he murmured. 'Does this Sheri have a sister? A sister whose husband also died?'

'Yes, yes. So *did* you know Henu?' Isis was excited now. 'Was he killed in a big battle?'

Nes let his hands drop. 'No, he wasn't.' He sighed and got to his feet again.

'But if he didn't die in battle, what happened to him?' Isis demanded. She felt a bound of hope. 'Is he still alive?'

Nes shook his head. 'No. He is dead.' His eyes were full of sadness and he placed a hand gently on Isis's shoulder. 'Come. We must go to the camp. I have something to show you. These women have waited far too long to hear the truth.'

Djeri had drifted off to sleep again. Hopi decided it was time to leave. He needed to think, and besides, he still wanted to talk to Menna. Anty waved him off, thanking him once more, and he headed into the heat of the early afternoon sun.

Hopi wandered back towards his tutor's house, feeling unhappy. Of course, he had always known that the lives of soldiers were brutal. It was their job to kill and maim others, and to take prisoners, too – all for the protection of Egypt and the glory of their king. And it wasn't just the enemy that had a hard time; he had once overheard a group of soldiers describing the beatings they had received during training. Thinking about it now, he began to realise that he was lucky. A poor boy such as himself could easily have been conscripted, but his limp meant he was exempt. Then he thought of the terror in the Libyan's eyes as he had lifted the box containing the deathstalkers, and knew that this punishment was different. It was in a terrible class of its own.

He reached the far end of Menna's street. To his astonishment, he saw someone hammering on the priest's door. So Menna *still* wasn't back. And then he realised that the man was not a man of the town. His hair was cut in the style of a soldier and he was holding a spear like a staff.

Hopi quickened his pace. In frustration, the soldier gave the door a kick, then turned on his heel and began to run in the opposite direction.

'Wait!' he called, but the soldier was already turning the corner.

Looking around wildly, Hopi spotted a group of boys playing catch with a leather ball. 'Which of you can run fast?' he demanded.

'I can! I can!' chorused the boys.

'Then run,' ordered Hopi. 'Catch the soldier who was banging on Menna's door. Go, now! As fast as you can!'

The boys set off in a cloud of dust, their bare feet thundering. Hopi limped as far as his tutor's door and crouched against the wall to wait. Where was Menna? He wondered. And what did the soldier want?

A jabber of voices soon heralded the boys' return. They turned the corner, the soldier in their midst clearly angry and confused.

'Who ordered my return?' demanded the soldier. 'I have not a minute to lose!'

Hopi stood to greet him. 'I did. Who are you seeking?' he asked.

'Menna, the priest of Serqet,' the soldier replied. 'We were told that he is the greatest in the town. Has he returned? It's urgent – desperate!'

'No,' Hopi told him. 'But I am his apprentice. What's happened?'

'It's the commander. He's been stung by a scorpion – a deathstalker! His cries have filled the camp with terror, his shrieks are like those of an animal, a jackal.'

Hopi's mouth dropped open.

'I cannot wait any longer – I must find another priest.' The soldier was already pulling away from the boys, distracted and sweaty.

'I will come.' Hopi's mind was working fast. 'I know the spells. But I must somehow enter Menna's house for some herbs. This is the quickest solution, I can assure you.'

'But the house is shut,' objected the soldier. 'I can't waste any more time.'

Hopi looked up at the walls. 'I know how to enter,' he said. 'Menna will understand. Wait here.'

Around the side of the house were steps leading up to the roof. They were rarely used, as the mud brick was crumbling. Hopi limped up them, hopping over the broken brickwork, and clambered on to the roof. From there, he jumped awkwardly down the steps that led into the courtyard. Hopi tried the house door. Menna hadn't bothered to bar it, and so he half-ran, half-limped to the sanctuary where Menna kept his supply of herbs.

This was where they had sat chanting the night before. Hopi reached for the herbs that Menna had shown him and went to stuff them into his bag. Then he slapped his forehead – but of course, he didn't have his bag! It hadn't been in the sanctuary when he had woken up that morning. Hopi dashed to the door. Menna must have put it in the front room, where he had slept. But then he stopped in his tracks. There was the bag, sitting by the doorway with the papyrus basket inside. He frowned. He was *sure* it hadn't been there when he had woken up.

There was no time to puzzle over it now. He grabbed the bag and shoved the herbs inside, then slung it over his shoulder and made his way out of the house the way he'd come. The soldier was waiting impatiently, shifting from one foot to another.

'Come on,' said Hopi. 'Let's go. I'll walk as fast as I can.'

CHAPTER NINE

Isis trotted after the great wrestler. She was bursting with questions, but it was all she could do to keep up with him. They hurried through the streets of Waset and beyond, to the area of parched desert that separated the town from the camp. The sun was fierce, but Nes did not slow down. He marched across the sea of sand and pebbles with his eyes fixed on the canvas of the camp, just visible in the shimmering haze.

Up ahead, the ground seemed to shift, blurring into the blue of a mirage. Isis was used to such tricks of the desert and ignored it at first. But then, emerging from the patch of reflected sky, she saw a figure. He was not on the track, but to one side of it, as though coming from the desert itself.

She stopped for a moment, shielding her eyes. All she could make out were swathes of linen, wrapped

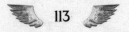

around the figure to protect him from the sun. He carried a spear. No, not a spear . . . Isis squinted in the harsh light. There was no bronze at the tip. It was simply a staff.

In alarm, she realised that Nes had not faltered. He was already well ahead, and Isis turned to run after him. 'Nes! Wait!' she cried, sprinting forward again.

The wrestler only turned one shoulder to beckon her. 'It's not far now!' he called. 'We shall soon be there!'

Isis threw one last glance at the stranger, who seemed to be making for Waset. Then she obeyed and ran at full tilt to catch up with the wrestler, keeping at his heels until they reached the boundary of the camp.

Something had happened. Isis sensed it at once. The soldiers were crowded together in groups, gossiping. It looked as though they had stopped mid-training; charioteers stood at their horses' heads, trying to calm them, as infantrymen stood idle with their bows and spears.

'Where are the officers?' demanded Nes, as they passed the first group. 'Why aren't you training?'

'They are all in the commander's tent!' a young soldier told him, pointing, his face alight with fear.

'Nes, have you not heard the news?'

'What news?'

'Meref has been attacked. A scorpion stung him. The men are saying that the gods are avenging themselves.'

Nes stopped in his tracks. 'Is this true?'

'Yes! Yes! They say he won't live, they say there is no cure.'

Isis was agog. 'A scorpion! We must fetch Menna at once – or even Hopi . . .'

But Nes was not listening. He was gazing in the direction of the commander's tent, deep in thought. Then a sigh escaped him and he shook his head. 'This is not our concern,' he said gruffly to Isis. 'We have things to do.' And he marched off purposefully – in the opposite direction.

Isis scampered after him. 'Why won't you go and see? My brother knows about such things – he is an apprentice to Menna, the priest of Serqet.'

Nes did not reply.

'But we could help,' Isis protested, more weakly this time.

For some reason, Nes was not going to get involved. She realised that they were heading to his tent. Other soldiers called out to him as he passed, but he ignored them all. They reached his rough canvas shelter and he ducked inside.

'Come in,' he invited her.

Isis pushed back the flap of fabric to enter his tent for a second time. In daylight, it appeared bigger, but now that she could take a good look, it seemed very bare and spartan. Nes might own a farm somewhere, but he carried with him the absolute minimum – his weapons, a mat to lay on the floor and a bundle of possessions, which was resting in one corner. That was it.

'Sit,' he told Isis, reaching for the bundle.

She settled herself on the mat, watching curiously as he rummaged through his belongings. He soon found what he was looking for. It was a little alabaster jewellery box, similar to ones owned by Sheri, Nefert and Kia. He lifted off the lid and dipped his fingers inside.

'Open your hand,' he said, reaching towards her with his fist clenched.

Isis did as he said. Nes held her gaze for a second, and then she felt something small drop into her palm. Two things. She looked down, and found that she was holding two tiny flies. They were made of pure gold.

She gasped. 'Oh!'

'Many years ago, these were given to Henu and his brother in arms, Userkaf. They symbolise the Order of the Golden Fly, and were awarded for bravery in battle,' said Nes. 'I have kept them safely until this day.'

Isis was still staring at the flies in disbelief. Now she looked up. 'But why didn't you send them to Sheri and Kia?' she demanded. 'All this time, and they have received nothing. They don't even know how their husbands died!'

An expression of suffering came over Nes's face. 'This is a painful story,' he said. 'And I wish only to tell it once. We must return to town, and I shall tell them face to face.'

Commander Meref was having a convulsion. His back arched and twisted, and his legs thrashed on the floor. His eyeballs had rolled to the back of his head so that only the whites showed, and his eyelids flickered furiously. But worst of all was his mouth – his lips were drawn back from his teeth, white froth dribbled down and a horrible gurgling sound emerged from his throat.

Hopi stood at the opening of his tent, aghast. None of the soldiers knew what to do. They were watching their commander with a mixture of fascination and terror.

'Hold him down!' ordered Hopi.

The soldiers looked at him in surprise as the

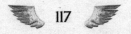

messenger led him inside.

'What is this boy doing here?' demanded one.

'I am the apprentice of Menna, the great priest of Serqet,' Hopi told them. He watched as the commander's arms flailed in the air. Blood joined the froth around his mouth – he had bitten his tongue. 'Please, do as I say! Hold him! And place a stick between his teeth, over his tongue.'

Something in his voice had an effect. Four of the men stepped forward and pinned the commander's limbs to the mat. His body juddered and bucked, but they held him fast, and another rammed a staff into his mouth.

'Nnngggghhhh,' gurgled the commander, his eyes still rolling wildly.

Hopi bent down and opened his bag. Fishing out the herbs, he looked up and barked, 'Bring me water, a bowl and a beaker. And some embers.'

While he waited, he knelt at the commander's head and placed his hands on his forehead. Closing his eyes, he began to chant the first of the spells he had learned only the night before. '*Blessed is Serqet, great goddess of poisons, blessed giver and taker of life, grant us your mercy . . . may the power of this poison be undone . . .*'

A soldier came running with a brazier, another

with the bowl and beaker. Crushing a handful of herbs into the bowl, Hopi continued to chant, then added water and placed the mixture over the smouldering coals. Strange, aromatic smells filled the tent.

The soldiers holding Meref began to tire, but in between the chanting, Hopi urged them on.

'Do not let him move! If your arms are weak, let your brothers help you!' he cried.

More soldiers piled in to hold the commander down. The convulsions came and went. Just when it seemed that his body was calm, another spasm would take hold, hurling his body this way and that. Hopi poured some of his potion into the beaker, and in the quieter moments, dribbled drops of it into the victim's mouth. He chanted and chanted again, losing all track of time.

At last, the commander lay still. Hopi had exhausted the spells. Everyone in the tent stared at the man who now lay prone on the floor. They were tensed and ready for the next convulsion. His eyes were now closed. He was quite unconscious.

Slowly, Hopi got to his feet.

'Will he live?' asked one of the men.

Hopi did not know the answer. 'I have done my best,' he replied. 'His life is in the hands of the goddess. All I can say is this: should he be spared, his recovery will be slow. He will suffer for weeks. You would do well to appoint another commander.'

Nes led Isis out of his tent. Then, to her surprise, he did not head out of the camp, but to a stand of several chariots. Their horses were tethered behind them, dozing in the mellowing sun. A soldier emerged from between them, holding a leather bridle in one hand and a cloth in the other. He looked young and gentler than many of the others.

'Nebnufer. I am glad to see that someone is doing some work around here,' commented the wrestler. 'I hope you can do me a favour.'

'Anything. You are the Lion,' said Nebnufer. 'I am one of your greatest fans.'

'Then you can drive us into town,' said Nes. 'The little dancer has walked enough today.'

Nebnufer noticed Isis standing behind Nes. He looked curious to see her, but didn't comment. 'Of course. I will prepare the horses at once.'

Isis felt a thrill of excitement as Nebnufer untethered two black stallions. The horses were spirited, one stamping backwards and the other rearing up as Nebnufer led them to the slender chariot. But the young soldier was not afraid. He calmed them with soothing noises and soon had them harnessed. Nes stepped up beside him and held out a hand for Isis.

'Hold on tight,' he instructed her, and Isis grasped the side of the chariot.

It began to move and Isis gasped. It was much more bumpy than she'd imagined. She gripped tighter as they picked up speed through the camp, clinging on as they swayed and jolted over the rough terrain. Then they were out on the desert plain and the horses broke into a canter. Isis felt the wind whip past her, bringing tears to her eyes, and her whole body felt as though it were being shaken to pieces.

At the edge of Waset, Nebnufer slowed the horses down. Isis gave directions, and soon they were winding through the back streets, along alleys that were barely wide enough for the two horses. Then they were on her street, and to her delight, she saw Mut running to meet them.

'Isis! Isis! We've been looking for you!' cried her dance partner, her eyes wide with wonder.

Her calls brought Sheri to the door of the house, soon followed by Kia, holding little Kha in her arms. Isis watched the expressions on the two women's faces as the chariot came to a halt, and how they changed from curious to disbelieving – to stunned.

Nes lifted Isis down from the chariot, then jumped

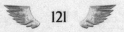

down himself. 'Wait for me,' he instructed Nebnufer.

Isis took the great wrestler's hand. 'Come inside.' She looked at the expectant faces of the family. 'Nes has something to show you,' she told them. She led him across the threshold and into the front room. 'Please sit, Nes,' she said, offering a stool.

'Would you like some fresh beer?' asked Sheri.

'And some figs?' Isis added playfully.

Nes smiled. 'Fresh beer sounds good,' he said. 'Thank you.'

Ramose appeared and gazed at Nes with solemn admiration. 'Are you a soldier?' he demanded. 'I want to be one. I want to chop up Libyans.'

'Ramose! Go and play in the courtyard,' Kia chided him. She put Kha down. 'And take your brother with you.'

Ramose pouted in disappointment as Paneb and Nefert joined the gathering. Everyone waited in silence until Sheri reappeared with the beer. And then, bursting with the news, Isis made her announcement.

'Sheri, Nes knew Henu,' she said. 'Look. His dagger is the same as the one you showed me. That's how I worked it out!'

Sheri almost dropped the pitcher of beer. She sat down heavily on a stool. 'What?'

'And your husband, too, Kia,' Isis carried on happily. 'What was his name again? User—'

'Userkaf.' Kia's voice was faint.

'Please tell them, Nes,' said Isis. 'And show them what you showed me.'

Slowly, the wrestler's hand moved to the pouch he had slung around his waist. He removed it, then he reached for the dagger and lifted that from its scabbard. He lay the dagger on the floor at his feet, then reached inside the pouch and brought out the little box that he had shown Isis. Then he looked across at Kia.

'You were Userkaf's wife?' he asked.

Kia was staring at the dagger. 'I was,' she whispered.

'Then this now belongs to you.' Nes turned the hilt of the dagger so that it faced towards her. 'Take it, for Userkaf would have wanted you to receive it.'

Kia dropped from her stool on to her knees. She buried her face in her hands for a moment. Then, silently, she reached for the dagger and picked it up, turning it over and over in her hands.

'What . . . what happened to them?' It was Sheri who spoke. 'Can you tell us that?'

Nes looked troubled. 'I can,' he said. 'But it may not be what you wish to hear. First, let me give you these.' Carefully, he opened the box and scooped up the flies. Then he turned his hand over, so that the gold glinted in his palm.

Everyone leaned forward to look.

'Golden flies – for valour!' Paneb's voice was full of awe.

'One was awarded to Henu, the other to Userkaf,' said Nes. 'I took them into safe keeping when they were both lying on their deathbeds. I was given Userkaf's dagger at the same time.'

'Who killed them?' Kia's voice was hoarse.

Nes sighed heavily. 'It was not the enemy you imagine. They were not killed in battle at all, but by the goddess Sekhmet.'

'*Sekhmet?*' Sheri sounded full of fear. 'But what did they do to deserve that?'

'Do not think this way. Sekhmet's actions are beyond reason. Her greed for life sometimes over-comes everything else. She can sweep the land with destruction in her paws and pestilence in her breath.'

Pestilence. Of course. The great lioness was not only the goddess of war. Isis saw how the soldier was trying to break the news gently, but now she realised the truth. The men had been struck down by sickness.

'Go on,' said Kia.

Nes took a deep breath, then plunged into his story. 'We were in the north, picking off groups of invaders. They were ill equipped, badly trained, and we had no difficulty in dealing with them. But what they lacked in weapons, they made up for with something else. They brought among us a plague – a terrible plague.' Involuntarily, he shuddered. 'One after one, the men were struck down. Our camp became like the worst of battlegrounds, but the enemy we fought was invisible.'

'How dreadful.' Nefert spoke softly.

'And this is how they died?' asked Sheri quietly.

Nes nodded. 'Yes. I was among the last to suffer the sickness. I went around speaking to my fellows, offering what comfort I could. I did not know Henu and Userkaf well, but I knew they had fought together bravely in many battles. And as they lay dying, they entrusted their golden flies and the dagger to me. They told me your names. But then I, too, was taken sick.'

'You lived.' Kia's voice shook.

'Yes. I was one of the few. But when I began to recover, my mind was confused. It took me several weeks to regain my strength. The survivors were too few to give the dead the treatment they should have received. They were buried in the sand, in the hope that the gods would heal them in the Next World.'

'And us? Why did you not come and find us?' asked Sheri.

'Try as I might, I could not remember your names. Henu and Userkaf were dead. Most of their platoon was also dead, and I was weak . . .' Nes paused, his brow furrowed. Then he sighed, and carried on, 'Time passed. We stayed in the north for many months, slowly rebuilding the company. I took to wearing the dagger, in memory of those we had lost. I gave up hope of ever returning it to its true owner.'

'But you have found us at last,' said Sheri. 'It is a miracle for which I shall be forever thankful.' She clutched her golden fly to her chest and burst into tears.

CHAPTER TEN

Hopi gathered what was left of the herbs and placed them back in his bag. As he did so, he brushed his hand over his papyrus basket, and felt himself flush. What if these soldiers knew what he had inside? Hurriedly, he slung the bag over his shoulder.

'Thank you, young priest,' said an officer. 'Tell me, how can we repay you?'

'Oh.' Hopi hadn't thought of that. It was usually Menna who dealt with such things. He thought for a moment, and remembered the young Libyan, terrified and tied to a stake in the centre of the pit. Perhaps he could do something for him. 'You have a prisoner,' he said.

The officer smiled. 'We have more than a hundred prisoners.'

'I mean, there's one particular prisoner. He tried to

escape and he was sent to the pit.'

The officer immediately looked suspicious. 'How do you know about that?' he demanded. He took a step towards Hopi. 'Who told you about the pit?'

'No one. I mean . . .' Hopi thought quickly. 'My sister is one of the dancers who visited you. She told me what happened while she was here.'

The officer narrowed his eyes and took another step towards Hopi. 'Don't I recognise you?' he demanded. 'Weren't you here with her last night?'

'No. I mean, yes.' Hopi was sweating. He didn't know what to say. 'Yes. But I left with the troupe.'

The officer shook his head. 'No, I don't think you did. I don't remember seeing you then and I have a very good memory.' He stroked his chin. 'Something went missing in the course of the evening,' he said. 'Do you know what that was?'

Hopi bowed his head. 'Yes, I know,' he managed to say. 'I heard that you lost your scorpions.'

The officer was studying him carefully. There was silence, and Hopi realised that all the officers were staring at him now.

'*You* seem to know a lot about them,' said one of them casually.

Hopi's heart started to yammer inside his chest. He thought of the deathstalkers lying in the depths of his basket, and wondered what the officers would do to him if they found them. But then he realised they had no reason to suspect him. He had helped the commander. He had acted as Menna would have wanted him to, and he drew himself up taller.

'Yes, I know a lot about them,' he said. 'I am a servant of the goddess Serqet. I also know what you used those scorpions for, and see what has befallen your commander! Her creatures should never have been used in that way. Now see the power of her curse!' He pointed down at Commander Meref. As they watched, his body twitched and juddered, but he did not regain consciousness.

The threatening officer stepped back, now looking afraid.

'The boy is right,' muttered another. 'We knew that this displeased the gods.'

'Serqet has spoken,' announced Hopi. 'The charioteer Djeri also acknowledges that he has been punished.'

'Djeri! You have seen him?' the officer gasped. 'Is he alive?'

'I have been treating his injuries,' said Hopi. 'The goddess has spared him, but he will be scarred for life.'

The officers looked stunned.

'This boy knows too much,' exclaimed one. 'He wields too much power. I, for one, will accept what he has to say.'

'And I also,' said another.

A ripple of agreement spread around the tent.

'What must we do to halt the wrath of the goddess?' asked the first.

Hopi considered his words carefully. 'From now on, your prisoners must be treated fairly. The pit must cease to exist,' he said, then paused. 'What has become of that Libyan?'

'He is still awaiting punishment,' an officer answered.

'The terror he has endured is punishment enough,' said Hopi. 'Please return him to his fellow prisoners. If he has relatives, make sure that their fate is decided together, and is a just one.'

The men around him looked at each other.

'Is that all?' asked one.

Hopi nodded. 'Yes.'

He watched as relief spread slowly over their faces. It was nothing compared to the relief that he was feeling himself, but he tried not to let it show.

He turned to go. 'I must leave you now. I will return tomorrow. By then, you can be sure of the commander's destiny one way or the other.'

A guard escorted Hopi to the edge of the camp,

and he set off for Waset as the afternoon sun began to drift towards the west. Before reaching the entrance to the town, he stopped and looked around. There was a rocky area just off the track and he walked towards it. It was time the deathstalkers were given their freedom.

He crouched down and opened his bag, then lifted out his basket. Taking great care, he pulled off the lid and tipped the basket on one side, then waited for the scorpions to appear. Nothing happened. Hopi frowned and gave the basket a little shake. Still nothing. Curious, he picked it up and peered inside.

There was nothing there. The basket was completely empty.

From the roof, Isis and Hopi stared out over the darkening sky, sharing a bowl of raisins between them.

'I can't believe you were *there*,' said Isis. 'Right there in the camp. Nes wouldn't go and see the commander – he took me straight to his tent for the golden flies.'

'Maybe he was wise not to,' said Hopi. 'Maybe he wants nothing to do with him. It sounds as though Nes is a good man.'

'Yes, he is good,' agreed Isis. 'Imagine, he kept the flies all those years. Sheri and Kia have spent most of the day crying, but they are happy, I think.'

Hopi nodded. 'They must be.'

Isis handed the rest of the raisins to her brother. She'd had enough. The day's events had given her butterflies, and there was still more to come. Nes had invited her back to the camp to witness the distribution of the prisoners of war, and though she didn't know whether to look forward to it or dread it, at least horrible Commander Meref would be in no fit state to make their lives any more miserable.

'Could you come with me tomorrow?' she asked her brother. 'Back to the camp, I mean?'

'I have to go back to see the commander,' said Hopi.

'So we can go together!' Isis was delighted.

'Well, maybe. I'll need to talk to Menna first.' Hopi frowned. 'It's very odd, the way I haven't seen him all day. I hope nothing's wrong. And it's odd that my basket was empty, too.'

Suddenly, Isis remembered something. 'Hopi,' she said slowly, 'I think I may have seen him.'

'You? Where? Was he in town?'

Isis shook her head. 'No. On my way out to the camp, I saw an old man in the distance.' The more she thought about it, the more she was convinced. 'I'm sure it was Menna.'

'Menna, out in the desert? But why?'

'You tell me, Hopi.' Isis looked at him. 'Don't you think it was him who took the deathstalkers? Maybe he was releasing them out there.'

'But he wouldn't have had to go so far to do that.' A strange look came into her brother's eyes, and she saw that he was having the same thought as herself.

'You don't think he . . .' Isis felt a thud of shock.

'He couldn't have.' Hopi seemed just as flabbergasted.

'He could, Hopi.'

Hopi shook his head. 'But . . .'

Isis saw the first star appear in the sky above Waset. 'He was all wrapped in linen against the sun and carrying his staff. It wouldn't have been that difficult for an old man like him to get into the camp. He could have pretended to be sick, or perhaps a wandering prophet.'

Hopi looked thoughtful. 'I would never have imagined such a thing.'

Isis shrugged. 'Well, think about it,' she said. 'Maybe he felt that Serqet needed a helping hand.'

Hopi woke at first light. He had much to do before going back to the camp with Isis, and first on his list was a visit to Menna. Surely Isis was wrong. Surely his tutor could not have taken the affairs of the gods into his own hands like that?

The rest of the family was still sleeping. Quietly, he went down to the courtyard and splashed some water on to his face, then slipped out into the street. To his relief, his tutor's door yielded to his push, and he let himself in. The first shafts of sunlight had just reached the courtyard, and Menna sat there cross-legged, basking in its rays.

'Menna,' said Hopi. 'You're back. I looked for you all day yesterday.'

The old man nodded. 'Yes. And I hear you were busy in my absence.'

'You heard what happened? But how?'

Menna smiled. 'You know very well not to ask such questions, Hopi.'

Hopi settled himself on the mats next to his tutor. 'But . . .' He shook his head, frustrated. 'Admit that you released the deathstalkers, at least.'

'I did.'

'In the army camp? It was you, wasn't it?'

But Menna wouldn't be drawn. 'I spent some time in the desert,' was all he would say. He touched Hopi's arm. 'Don't get too comfortable there. I want you to get up again in a minute.'

Hopi gazed at him. 'Menna, tell me, please!'

The old man's wise, far-seeing eyes met his. 'You

did well yesterday, Hopi. I am proud of you. You are well on the way to entering the priesthood of Serqet.'

'Thank you. I hope I shall serve her well.' Hopi felt a thrill at Menna's words, but he also knew, now, that his tutor would never admit where he had been the day before. Resigned, he got to his feet. 'I shall do your bidding. I should hurry, because I've agreed to go back to check on the commander later.'

Menna nodded. 'Your errand should not take you too long. I want you to check on Djeri's progress – and I want you to tell him something. Tell him that I am renewing the offer I made many years ago.'

'The offer? What offer?' Hopi was baffled.

'He will know exactly what I mean.'

Hopi thought back to the awful scene with Djeri the day before. He still didn't know how to feel about it. 'Very well,' he said. 'But you know that it was he who caught Commander Meref's deathstalkers?'

Menna sighed. 'Yes, I know.'

'But how could he do such a thing, Menna? I wanted to think well of him, but how can I, when he did that?'

The old priest looked thoughtful. 'You are right to ask, Hopi. It is true that he strayed off the path, and the goddess was forced to punish him. But there is still hope for young Djeri. He understands what he has done, and he is sorry for it. What he needs now is not more suffering, but guidance.'

Suddenly, Hopi had an inkling as to what the offer might be. His heart lifted, for if Menna could forgive Djeri, then so could he. 'You are giving him a second chance.'

'You will see. Go now,' said Menna. 'And may the gods go with you.'

Hopi left and hurried to Djeri's house. He found the soldier sitting up, eating a breakfast of bread and dates. He looked up as Hopi came in.

'Welcome,' Djeri greeted him.

'You're looking better,' commented Hopi. 'How does the leg feel?'

'It itches,' said the soldier.

Hopi smiled. 'Well, don't scratch, whatever you do. I'll check it for you when you've finished eating.' He sat down and watched as Djeri polished off a flat loaf and popped another date into his mouth. 'I have come with a message from Menna.'

Djeri stopped chewing and looked at him warily. 'Is that so?'

'He says . . . he says he is renewing the offer that he made to you, many years ago.'

The soldier swallowed, then sat very still. Hopi waited for what seemed like a long time. At last, Djeri spoke. 'What do you think?' he asked.

Hopi shrugged. 'I don't know what he offered you. Though I think I can guess.'

The soldier grimaced. 'He asked me to become an apprentice priest of Serqet. Like you.'

'I thought as much.' Hopi nodded. 'And you turned him down.'

'Yes. I didn't want to sit studying herbs and potions,' said Djeri. 'I wanted to be a man of action. Marching, horses, the heat of battle . . . I love it.' He paused, and his expression grew sad. 'I loved it, I mean.'

Hopi understood, then, that Djeri had accepted his fate. He knew that he would never return to the army. 'So will you say yes?' he asked.

Djeri looked at him. 'I suppose it will mean working with you, won't it?'

'I'm afraid so.'

The soldier extended his hand to Hopi. 'Well,' he said. 'It seems that my fate is linked to Serqet, whatever my wishes may have been. I will say yes to Menna. And there are some compensations – I will be glad to call you my brother, and my friend.'

The atmosphere in the camp had changed overnight. Isis noticed it immediately. The sense of shock had been replaced with a buzz of excitement, and something in the air had lifted. She stood at the edge of the arena, listening to laughter and chatter as the soldiers began to gather. In the absence of Commander Meref, his second in command had taken control and was approaching the arena with an entourage of fellow officers. The chatter quietened down, and Isis glanced up at Nes standing by her side.

'Is it going to start?' she asked.

Nes nodded. 'Yes. As soon as the officers are seated, they will start bringing the prisoners.'

Isis felt nervous. She wasn't sure how much she really wanted to see people being handed out as property, but at the same time, she was too curious not to – especially where Neith and her brother were concerned.

The officers sat down. A pair of trumpets sounded and the second in command stood up.

'Company of Amun, servants of the king,' he began, 'you have fought well in recent weeks. Some of you have shown exceptional bravery. For that, you will be rewarded. But before our ceremony begins, I have an announcement to make.'

He paused and seemed to be gauging the soldiers' mood. Isis saw that they were listening intently, but without hostility.

'Commander Meref can no longer serve us,' said the second in command, and a murmur rippled through the assembly of soldiers. 'It is my duty to take his place.'

As he carried on speaking, someone nudged Isis, and she turned round quickly. It was Hopi.

'How is the commander?' she whispered. 'Is he dead?'

Hopi shook his head. 'Not dead. But much weakened,' he whispered back. 'He is lucky to be alive.'

'Thanks to you and your spells,' said Isis.

Hopi looked wry. 'I suppose so. I'm not sure he deserved them.'

'You did your duty,' said Isis. 'You must always do that.'

The trumpets sounded again, and now Isis saw movement. The prisoners were approaching, escorted by guards. She felt almost sick with nerves. A scribe stepped forward and began to recite a list of soldiers: those who had fought bravely, those who were injured, those who had won awards and those who would receive slaves. It seemed to take for ever. The prisoners had come to a halt, and Isis craned her neck to see if she could spot Neith, but all she could see were men. She couldn't even see Neith's brother.

At last the allocations began, and the prisoners

were shuffled forward into the arena. Isis saw that the male prisoners had been divided up. There was now not one group, but three, with the women in a cluster behind them.

'What do the groups mean?' she whispered to Nes.

He bent down to speak to her. 'The strongest will be trained as soldiers. They will serve with us in the army,' he said. 'The second group will be sent to the quarries to work. The third group will become personal slaves – that's reserved for old men and women.'

Isis felt a cold hand clutch her heart. So Neith was going to lose her brother, one way or another. She imagined being separated from Hopi and wanted to cry. Then the scribe caught her attention.

'Where is Nes, the Lion?' he called.

Nes raised his hand. 'I am here.'

'Nes, as always, you have excelled yourself in battle,' said the scribe. 'Another slave is yours for the taking. Make your choice.'

Nes stepped forward and addressed his fellow soldiers. 'Thank you, comrades.' He surveyed the slaves for only a second. 'I have no doubt who to choose. I shall take the girl Neith. Where is she?'

Isis gasped. So Neith would end up on Nes's farm! She didn't know whether to be happy or sad. She knew that the farming life was hard, especially for a girl on her own, but surely Nes would treat her kindly.

The guards separated Neith out from the other women and she was pushed to the fore. Isis gazed at her sorrowfully. And then she realised that Nes was still speaking.

'. . . But I don't wish to keep her for myself. Long ago, I knew two soldiers who fought bravely and died on duty. Their wives have waited many years for a reward. And so Neith shall go to them, as their handmaiden.'

Isis gripped Hopi's arm. She couldn't believe it. Neith was going to Sheri and Kia . . . ?

'That means she'll be living with *us*!' she breathed.

The scribe was busy noting it down. Then he frowned. 'I'm not sure that's possible,' he said.

Isis felt her heart was in her mouth. Surely there couldn't be a problem?

'By ordination of the priest of Serqet, this girl's brother must be allocated at the same time,' announced the scribe.

'That's easily resolved,' said Nes. 'Her brother is young and spirited. He is to become a soldier. But I will care for him personally and I'll supervise his training myself. And he shall receive the same rights as any of us to see his family.'

The scribe glanced across at the new commander. 'Do you agree to this, sir?'

Isis watched the man's face. He was clearly trying to make up his mind.

'Yes, it seems fair to me,' he responded eventually.

Isis let out a sigh of relief. She looked over at Neith, and smiled. It wouldn't be easy for her, a stranger in a new land. It wouldn't be easy for her brother, either, fighting with Egypt's great army. But at least there was some comfort for them. They were being allowed to settle here, and both were in good hands. Perhaps, in time, their future would be bright, after all.

CAST OF CHARACTERS

CHRONICLE CHARACTERS

Hopi The thirteen-year-old brother of Isis. Ever since surviving the bite of a crocodile in the attack that killed their parents, Hopi has had a fascination for dangerous creatures, particularly snakes and scorpions. He is training to be a priest of Serqet, which will qualify him to treat bites and stings.

Isis The eleven-year-old sister of Hopi. She is a talented dancer and performs regularly with Nefert and Paneb's troupe. Her dance partner is Mut.

Mut The eleven-year-old daughter of Paneb and Nefert, and dance partner to Isis.

Paneb Husband of Nefert, father of Mut, Ramose and Kha, and the head of the household where Isis and Hopi live. He organises bookings for the dance and music troupe.

Nefert Wife of Paneb, mother of Mut, Ramose and Kha, and sister of Sheri and Kia. She plays the lute and is head of the dance and music troupe.

Sheri One of Nefert's widowed sisters, and a musician in the troupe. She has a particularly loving nature.

Kia The second of Nefert's widowed sisters, also a musician living with the troupe. She is slightly more cold and distant than Sheri, but is hardworking and practical.

Ramose Eldest son of Nefert and Paneb, aged five. Mut's brother.

Kha Younger son of Nefert and Paneb, aged two. Mut's brother.

Menna Hopi's tutor, and a priest of Serqet in the town of Waset. (A priest of Serqet was someone who treated snake bites and scorpion stings.)

OTHER CHARACTERS IN THIS STORY

Neith A Libyan girl who hopes to find a new life with her brother in Egypt.

Anty A wealthy scribe in the town of Waset. He has three sons. His third son, Djeri, belonged to the army.

Djeri (you say 'Jerry') Son of Anty, and a charioteer in the army.

Commander Meref The commander of a company of the Amun division in the king's army.

Mose, the Great Bull A soldier in the Amun division, with a fearsome reputation for wrestling.

Nes, the Lion One of the oldest soldiers in the Amun division, and a famous wrestler.

Nebnufer A skilled horseman and chariot driver in the army.

Henu The former husband of Sheri, and a soldier in the army.

Userkaf The former husband of Kia, and a soldier in the army.

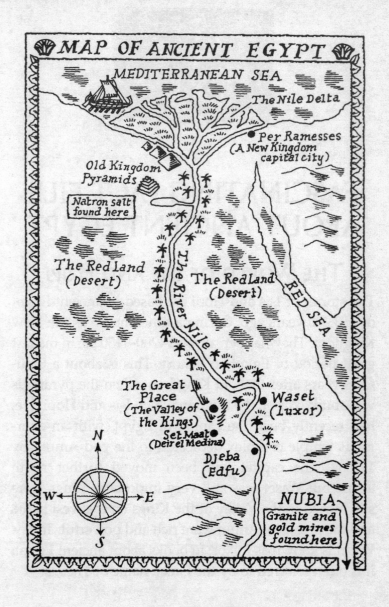

FASCINATING FACT FILE
ABOUT ANCIENT EGYPT

The World of Isis and Hopi

The stories of Isis and Hopi are based in ancient Egypt over 3,000 years ago, during a time known as the New Kingdom. They happen around 1200–1150 BC, in the last great period of Egyptian history. This is about a thousand years after the Old Kingdom, when the pyramids were built. Waset, the town in which Isis and Hopi live, had recently been the capital of Egypt, with an enormous temple complex dedicated to the god Amun. By 1200 BC, the capital had been moved further north again, but Waset was still very important. Kings were still buried in the Valley of the Kings on the west bank, and the priests of Amun were rich and powerful. Today, Waset is known as Luxor; in books about ancient Egypt, it is often referred to by the Greek name of Thebes.

A Little Bit about Scorpions

Scorpions belong to the order of creatures called arachnids. You've probably seen another kind of arachnid plenty of times – did you know that spiders are arachnids, too? Like spiders, scorpions have eight legs and an outer shell called an exoskeleton. But all scorpions have something else as well: they have a pair of pincers, and a tail with a venomous sting at the end.

So does that mean that all scorpions are danger-ous? Well, only if you're the sort of bug that a scor-pion likes to eat. Most scorpions' venom isn't strong enough to harm humans. There are about 1,500 dif-ferent kinds of scorpion, but only about 25 are known to have killed people. It just so happens that two of the most dangerous scorpions in the world live in Egypt. They are the two that Menna shows Hopi – the fat-tailed scorpion and the deathstalker.

A scorpion's venom contains something called neurotoxins, which attack a victim's nervous system. Human victims of deathstalkers and fat-tailed scorpions have symptoms like Commander Meref's – convulsions, paralysis, difficulty breathing and intense pain. Sometimes, the victim dies of heart failure. Most healthy adults pull through, but it's also true that approximately 5,000 people die of scorpion stings every year around the world.

The ancient Egyptians had a healthy respect for these dangerous creatures, and the scorpion goddess Serqet was worshipped throughout the land. Another version of her name means roughly 'she who paralyses the throat', so the Egyptians knew all about the effects of scorpion stings! Like many of the Egyptian gods, she had a double-sided nature: she could punish people, but she could prevent bites and stings, and bring healing, too.

THE ANCIENT EGYPTIAN ARMY

During the New Kingdom, the Egyptian army was very well organised, and was made up of 20,000 soldiers. The head of the army was the king himself, and he led his men into battle with major enemies. Most of the time, though, he left the day-to-day running of his troops to the commanders.

The army had four divisions of 5,000 men, each named after an important god: Amun, Ptah, Seth and Re. These divisions in turn had 20 companies, each with 250 men, and every company was divided into 5 platoons of 50 men. So the company that appears in this book is only a fraction of the whole Egyptian army.

The army could offer a good career for Egyptian

men, especially if they came from a wealthy family and had some education. Men like Djeri, the son of a scribe, might be able to progress through the ranks and end up being a commander. There were plenty of perks to be had, too. The king made sure that soldiers were rewarded for bravery with land, gold and slaves. It's strange but true that a golden fly was a particular reward for valour. We don't know exactly why, but it might be because flies are tough little creatures that never give up. Think of a fly buzzing at the window – it just keeps going and going . . .

But life in the army wasn't all rewards and excitement. For the average soldier, it could be very hard. Foot soldiers were often beaten by their superiors, and had to live in harsh conditions and march long distances. They also had to go through a tough physical regime of weapons training, fitness training and wrestling. And of course, they might become sick, injured or get killed.

It's also true that much of the army wasn't made up of Egyptians at all. There were whole platoons of other nationalities; for example, the Nubian platoon that forms part of the company in this book. Prisoners of war were regularly drafted into the army – and they seem to have been surprisingly loyal to the Egyptian king.

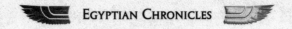
WHO WERE THE LIBYANS?

The Libyans were a group of tribes who came from the lands west of Egypt. They were usually portrayed in Egyptian wall paintings with beards and colourful robes. They were known to the Egyptians by a number of different names – the Libu, the Temehu and the Meshwesh, for example. They were a big nuisance for a number of New Kingdom kings, who had to keep trying to repel them from Egypt's borders. However, given that Egypt was a lush land of plenty, I have reinterpreted this a little bit; the Egyptians saw the Libyans as threatening invaders, but I have imagined that they envied the rich lands of Egypt and simply wanted to settle there. In fact, many of them did settle in Egypt. Some descendants of Libyan captives became important members of Egyptian society, and later on in Egyptian history, one of them even became king.

GODS AND GODDESSES

Ancient Egyptian religion was very complicated. There wasn't just one god, but hundreds, each symbolising something different. Many of them were linked to a particular animal or plant. The Egyptians believed that their king or pharaoh was one of the gods, too.

Not everyone worshipped the same gods. It would have been very difficult to worship all of them, because there were so many. Some gods were more important than others, and some places had special gods of their own. People would have had their favourites depending on where they lived and what they did.

These are some of the most important gods of the New Kingdom, and all the special ones that are mentioned in this book.

Ammut A monster who waited in the Next World to gobble the hearts of people who had not led a good life. She had the head of a crocodile, the front paws of a lion and the hindquarters of a hippopotamus.

Amun The great god of Waset (Thebes), a creator god and god of the air. When Waset became very powerful in the New Kingdom, he was combined with the sun god Re and became **Amun-Re**. He was shown with tall feathers on his head, or with a ram's head.

Anubis The god of mummies and embalming. He was usually shown with a jackal's head.

Bes A god who was worshipped in people's homes, rather than at shrines and temples. He was shown as a bearded dwarf, often with his tongue sticking out, and was believed to protect people's houses, pregnant women and children.

Hathor A goddess of fertility, love, music and dancing. She was usually shown as a cow, or a woman with a cow's head, or a woman with a cow's ears and horns.

Horus The falcon-headed king of the gods, who fought and won a battle with his evil uncle Seth. The reigning king of Egypt was believed to be the embodiment of Horus.

Isis The mother of Horus and wife of Osiris, the goddess of motherhood and royal protection. She was associated with the goddess Hathor.

Khepri The scarab god, the god of the rising sun. It was believed that he pushed the sun up every morning in the same way that a scarab pushes its ball of dung.

Khonsu The moon god of Waset, worshipped in the great temple complex there. He was the adopted son of Mut.

Ma'at The goddess of truth and justice, balance and order, who helped to judge people's hearts after their death.

Mut The great mother goddess of Waset, worshipped with Amun and Khonsu. Because Waset is often called Thebes, these three are known as the 'Theban Triad'.

Osiris Husband of Isis, father of Horus and brother of the evil god Seth. He was the king of the underworld, so he was usually shown as a mummy.

Ptah A creator god, and the god of craftsmen. He was usually shown as a mummy holding a symbolic staff.

Re (or **Ra**) The sun god, who travelled across the sky every day in a *barque* (boat).

Sekhmet The lioness goddess of war, destruction and disease. She could offer protection and healing from these evils, too, and it was believed that she offered special protection to the king.

Serqet The goddess of scorpions. She was believed to cure the stings and bites of all dangerous creatures like snakes and scorpions.

Seth The brother of Osiris, the god of chaos, evil and the Red Land (the desert). He was shown with the head of a strange dog-like creature that has never been identified.

Sobek The ancient Egyptian crocodile god. On the whole, he was feared by the Egyptians, but he was sometimes seen as a god of fertility, too.

Tawaret A hippopotamus goddess who protected children and women, particularly during childbirth. Like Bes, Tawaret was worshipped in people's homes rather than in temples.

Thoth The god of writing and scribes. He was shown as an ibis, or with the head of an ibis.

GLOSSARY

acacia A small, thorny tree. Some types of acacia grow particularly well in dry, desert regions.

alabaster A whitish stone that is quite soft and easily carved. The Egyptians used it to make many beautiful objects.

amulet A lucky charm, worn to protect a person from evil.

ankh The ancient Egyptian symbol of eternal life. It is a cross with a loop at the top. Amulets were made in this shape, and gods were shown holding an *ankh* in tomb paintings.

Black Land The rich, fertile land close to the Nile, where the ancient Egyptians felt safe. They lived and grew their crops here.

carob An evergreen shrub. Its seed pods are edible.

castor A shrubby plant widely grown in ancient Egypt. Its seeds were used to make castor oil, which the Egyptians rubbed on their skin and hair to make them

glossy, and burned as fuel in oil lamps.

golden fly A fly shaped in gold, and awarded to soldiers for valour. Golden flies have been found strung on to necklaces.

hieratic A shorthand version of hieroglyphics, which simplified the hieroglyphs to make them quicker to write.

hieroglyphics The ancient Egyptian system of picture writing. Each individual picture is called a **hieroglyph**.

Hittites Enemies of the Egyptians during the New Kingdom. They had a big empire to the north of Egypt and their capital was in modern-day Turkey.

Ipet-Isut The ancient Egyptian name for the great temple complex just to the north of Waset, now known as Karnak.

Ipet-Resyt The large temple complex in the town of Waset, connected to Ipet-Isut by a long avenue lined with sphinxes. Like Ipet-Isut, it was dedicated to the worship of Amun, Mut and Khonsu. It is now known as Luxor Temple.

jasper A popular gemstone in ancient Egypt. As well as green, there were red, brown, black and yellow varieties.

kohl A kind of dark powder that the Egyptians used as eyeliner to outline their eyes.

lotus Lotus flowers were actually blue water lilies that grew along the Nile. Their flowers open in the morning and close at night, so they were seen as a symbol of the rising and setting sun, and the cycle of creation. They were used in perfume, and were believed to have healing powers, too.

ma'at The ancient Egyptian principle of divine justice and order. The principle was represented by a goddess of the same name.

malachite A green-coloured mineral that the Egyptians used in cosmetics, jewellery and even medicinal remedies.

mercenary Someone who hires himself out as a soldier. Unlike most soldiers, who fight for their country or government, mercenaries fight for whoever is paying them.

natron A kind of salt mixture that was found on the bed of dried-up lakes in the desert. It was good at soaking up moisture, so it was used for drying out bodies in the embalming process. It was also used as an everyday cleaning agent.

Next World The place ancient Egyptians believed they would go after death. It would be better than this world, of course, but quite similar – which was why they needed to take their bodies and many possessions with them.

Nubian Someone from the region of Nubia, directly to the south of Egypt.

papyrus A kind of reed that used to grow in the marshes alongside the Nile, especially in the Delta region to the north. It was made into many things – mats, baskets, sandals and even boats – but it is most famous for the flat sheets of 'paper' made from it, which are named after the reed.

pharaoh The ancient Egyptian term for their king. It was only used by the Egyptians themselves in the later stages of their history, but we now use it to refer to any ancient Egyptian king.

Red Land The desert, the land of the dangerous god Seth. It was greatly feared by the Egyptians because it was impossible to live there.

scarab A kind of dung beetle that was worshipped by the Egyptians. Scarab amulets were thought to give great protection. The scarab was the creature of the god Khepri (see the Gods and Goddesses section).

Sea People The name given to waves of people who tried to invade Egypt from the Mediterranean Sea during the New Kingdom.

senet A popular board game in ancient Egypt. Players had to throw sticks to decide how many squares they could move their pieces.

side-lock The tuft of hair that boys kept long as part of their hairstyle. The rest of the head was shaved. Once they grew up, the side-lock was shaved off.

temple Temples were a very important focus for the ancient Egyptian religion. There were cult temples for the worship of a particular god, and mortuary temples for the worship of a king after his death.

terebinth A small tree that produces a substance called turpentine (a kind of resin with many uses).

turquoise A green-blue semi-precious stone that was mined by the Egyptians in Sinai. They used it to make beautiful objects, inlays and jewellery.

In case you missed their first exciting story,
read on for a tantalising taster of
Isis and Hopi's first adventure in

THE SPITTING COBRA . . .

EGYPTIAN CHRONICLES

THE SPITTING COBRA

In the flickering light of the oil lamp, the gold on the lid of the casket gave off a fiery glow. Nakht turned the precious object over in his hands, examining it closely. He opened the lid and peered inside; he ran his finger over the fine inlaid patterns of carnelian, lapis lazuli and gold.

'A very fine copy, don't you think?' asked Baki.

Nakht shook his head. 'This is no copy. I'd know it anywhere,' he said. 'I worked on it myself. And I placed it in the tomb with my own hands.'

Baki stroked his chin. 'You're sure?'

'By Horus and all the gods, I couldn't be more certain.'

Baki gave a heavy sigh. 'Then let us await the messenger.'

The two foremen lapsed into silence. Nakht placed the casket on the floor, and they gazed at it, as though it might be able to give them an answer to the mystery.

At last, there was a soft knock on the door. Nakht stood, and went to open it. A young man stepped inside, still breathless from running down the mountain.

'Well?' demanded Baki. 'What did you find?'

'The tomb has not been touched, sir,' replied the young man. 'The door is still in place, with the seals of the Great Place in perfect condition.'

Nakht sat down heavily, shaking his head. 'Impossible,' he murmured.

'You're sure you checked the right tomb?' queried Baki.

'Of course, sir,' said the messenger. 'I checked three times, and all the tombs nearby, just to be sure.'

The two foremen exchanged glances. The young man stood nervously, shifting from one foot to the other.

'You may go,' said Baki.

'Thank you, sir.' The messenger stepped quickly to the door, and disappeared into the night.

Nakht stood up again, and started pacing the room. 'So,' he said. 'This casket has been found in our village, but it belongs in a royal tomb. This much is sure. But the robbers are cunning. They did not break into the tomb via the doorway. They must have made another way in. It all points to one thing, Baki. The robbers live among us, here in Set Maat. No one else knows the mountain so well; no one else has the knowledge and skill to create another entrance.'

Baki ran a hand over his head, then once more stroked his jaw. 'This cannot be,' he muttered. 'I cannot believe that such a terrible thing has come among us.'

'There is no other explanation,' said Nakht, his face full of sorrow. 'We cannot hide from the truth. We must find the robbers, even if they are our relatives and friends. It is our sacred duty.'

'But how?'

Nakht sat down, rested his elbows on his knees and bowed his head. 'Yes, how,' he murmured.

The two men were not afraid of silence. They had known each other for many, many years. They sat and stared at the beautiful casket once more, each wondering whether the other would come up with an idea. At last, it was Nakht who spoke.

'The harvest approaches,' he said. 'Let us each throw a party. We can afford to be generous; let there be music and dancing and rich food and wine. Indeed, we must make sure the wine flows freely, for that is our key. Wine and good cheer encourage tongues to speak freely. Someone will say something that should have remained a secret.'

Baki smiled wryly. 'I am surprised at you, brother,' he said. 'I never thought I would live to see you encourage drinking and revelry.'

But Nakht remained serious. 'Perhaps so,' he said.

'But I never thought I would live to see such things happen in our midst. Do you think it a good idea?'

Baki spread his hands expressively, and shrugged. 'I can see nothing wrong with it,' he said. 'And vanity may play a part as much as flagons of wine. If a robber's wife has acquired sumptuous jewellery, she may be tempted to wear it.'

'Then let us go ahead. The sooner the better.'

'Well . . .' Baki frowned. 'It may not be so easy. There are a few problems.'

'Such as?'

'Our best music troupe cannot perform at the moment. Wab and her family have a sickness, and their finest young dancer has broken her arm.'

Nakht slapped his thigh impatiently. 'But there are others!'

'They are priestesses, brother,' Baki pointed out. 'Can we really call on them for such a purpose?' He paused. 'Perhaps it would be better to wait awhile.'

'No.' Nakht was determined. 'We have to carry out our plan now. Rumours are already spreading. If we cannot use our own troupe, we can hire another. Let us send messengers to Waset; there are plenty of performers there. I will pay for them out of my own pocket if I have to.'

Baki could find no other objections. He nodded slowly. 'You speak wisely,' he said. 'We cannot delay. Let us send messengers first thing tomorrow . . .'

ISIS AND HOPI PERFORM FOR THE
PHARAOH'S TOMB-BUILDERS NEAR
THE VALLEY OF THE KINGS, JUST
AS THE VILLAGERS FALL UNDER
SUSPICION FOR BREAK-INS AT
THE ROYAL TOMBS . . .

HOPI AND ISIS TRAVEL ALONG THE
RIVER NILE AND PIT THEIR WITS
AGAINST DANGEROUS ENEMIES. CAN
THEY SOLVE THE WEB OF INTRIGUE
BEFORE THEIR BOAT JOURNEY ENDS?

HOPI AND ISIS ARE PREPARING
FOR AN IMPORTANT FESTIVAL,
WHEN THEY UNCOVER A PLOT BY
A VILLAINOUS TAX COLLECTOR . . .

ISIS MUST DANCE FOR THE EGYPTIAN
ARMY, WHILE HOPI NEEDS TO HEAL
A SOLDIER'S BATTLE WOUNDS.
THEN HOPI SENSES A DARK SECRET
WITHIN THE ARMY CAMP . . .

To order direct from Bloomsbury Publishing visit www.bloomsbury.com/gillharvey
or call 020 7440 2475

BLOOMSBURY

www.bloomsbury.com